CLEMENTINE

BY ANN HOOD

PENGUIN WORKSHOP

PENGUIN WORKSHOP
An imprint of Penguin Random House LLC, New York

First published in the United States of America by Penguin Workshop,
an imprint of Penguin Random House LLC, New York, 2023

Visit us online at penguinrandomhouse.com.

Library of Congress Cataloging-in-Publication Data is available.

Manufactured in Canada

ISBN 9780593094105   10 9 8 7 6 5 4 3 2 1 FRI

Design by Taylor Abatiell

FOR MY DAUGHTER
ANNABELLE, ALWAYS

—AH

IN WHICH I WAKE UP

I know how it goes in the movies because we are . . . were . . . a movie-watching family. Every Saturday night. All the Disney classics, of course, and both *Parent Traps*— the original and the remake—and *Toy Story 1*, *2*, and *3* and any movies with horses or dogs in them. Mom usually slipped in one of her favorites for the second movie because she knew Halley almost always fell asleep by then, anyway. There would always be pizza during the first movie and popcorn during the second movie. We only got up from the couch to put the bag of popcorn in the microwave or get more drinks. It was the only night of the week that we were allowed soda, so even more special.

In the movies, the person—the main character, usually—wakes up from her coma and there are loving faces staring down at her. A nurse scurries out of the room to find a doctor. There are tears from the grateful family. *You're alive! You made it!*

Real life is very different from the movies. I should know this by now. In the movies, tragedy is averted, lives are saved, people get better and happier. In real life, when the main character—that would be me, Clementine Marsh, age fourteen and a half—opens her eyes, one of them kind of sticks halfway shut because there is some medical goop on them. Her throat is on fire from the tube they stuck down there in the OR and her leg aches from the big toe to the knee, like there's a tiny drummer in there banging away, hard.

"Thirsty," is the first thing I manage to say. It comes out like sandpaper.

There is no scurrying nurse, no grateful family. There is just Mom, looking exhausted.

"Oh, Clementine," she says in the saddest voice ever. "Why?"

Even if I could talk, I wouldn't be able to answer the

question. How can I ever explain what happened last night? What I was thinking and why I did what I did?

"Water," I croak instead.

Mom gets up and pours me some water from the mauve plastic pitcher by the bed. She sticks a straw in a cup and holds it to my lips while I sip, managing to stroke my hair with her free hand.

"I wish I knew what you were thinking," she says when I flop my head back down on the pillow.

I close my eyes again. They're scratchy, too. I try to imagine my whole body slowly turning into sandpaper, but Mom interrupts.

"You're in the psych ward," she whispers, like she's embarrassed.

My eyes fly open. "What? Why?"

"They're trying to find a place for you that's . . . nicer," Mom says. "I called Strawberry Fields, so maybe you can go back there."

I can't talk and I can't think straight. Psych ward? Strawberry Fields? What am I missing? I look at Mom's pretty, tired face for clues. But I only see worry and sadness. Her eyes are red from crying or not sleeping or both. She's got her hair pulled back in a messy ponytail and not a drop of makeup on.

Mom sighs and says, again, "Oh, Clementine. Why?"

Where do I even begin?

CHAPTER ONE

IN WHICH I START A NEW SCHOOL

THREE MONTHS EARLIER

My name is Clementine, and ever since my younger sister Halley died two years ago, I have not been right. Something is really wrong with me, with my heart and my mind and maybe even my soul, if we have souls. One typical autumn day when I was twelve and Halley was nine, we went to school at Morning Glory Montessori like we always did. We ate toasted frozen waffles in the car because we were running late. We forgot to kiss Mom goodbye because we were running late. We dropped into our seats in our different classes just before our teachers called our names in roll call because we were running late. "Here!" I could hear Halley respond from down the hall. "Here!" I answered my own teacher a nanosecond later.

Halley did her fourth-grade stuff—state capitals and long division and *Tuck Everlasting*—and I did my sixth-grade stuff—negative numbers and ancient Greece and *The Giver*. Then we went to the cafeteria and Halley sat with her friends at the NO PEANUT table and I went in the kitchen and made myself a peanut butter and jelly because school was the only place I could have one because of Halley's peanut allergy. While I was eating, my best friend Virginia talked about why cats were better than dogs and Luna talked about some new K-pop group and all of a sudden there was a big commotion, kids screaming and teachers running and from across the cafeteria Virginia's little sister Celeste screamed, "Clementine! It's Halley! Her peanut allergy!"

I went running so fast, but somehow the EMTs beat me to her. They were putting her on a stretcher and working on her at the same time and moving fast. "I'm her sister," I kept saying to them. And to Halley, "I'm right here. You're okay." Except she wasn't okay. And I haven't been okay, either, ever since.

Sometimes at night when I close my eyes I see comets and shooting stars exploding and no matter how hard I squeeze my eyes shut I can't make them go away. It's like my own personal Fourth of July on the backs of my eyelids. Although this may sound wonderful, let me tell you it is not. All I want to do is sleep and there are pyrotechnics in there.

Other times, it's sounds that I hear. Sounds like footsteps in the hall. Or a door opening and then closing very slowly. Or somebody breathing really close to me. If I sit up and shout *Get out!* my mother comes running in and turns on the light and says, "Oh, Clementine, what is it this time?" in a voice that is so sad and resigned and weary that I want to tell her it was just a bad dream. But Mom knows better. So I say *breathing* or *footsteps* or *door* or whatever it was and she sits on the bed next to me. Sometimes she takes my hand in her calloused ones. Sometimes she covers her face in her hands and bows her head and maybe cries or else tries not to cry.

Ever since Halley died, Mom has become an obsessive crafter, which is why her hands are calloused. From holding knitting needles and felting needles and hot glue guns; darning needles and crochet hooks and yarn and embroidery floss. She used to have soft hands, and these new, rough ones kind of freak me out. Like someone took over her body and replaced it with a hard shell. All the craft projects freak me out, too. Suddenly we have pillows with dumb sayings everywhere—*Be Your Own Kind of Beautiful! Bless This Mess! Naps Fix Everything!*—and miles of scarves and needlepointed kittens and tropical birds on junk-shop footstools.

If I manage to not shout and Mom doesn't know what I've heard, I might hyperventilate, so I keep brown paper lunch bags on my nightstand and breathe into them nice and slow. *Inhale and count to three and exhale and count to three. Inhale and count to three and exhale and count to three.* Over and over. Or I might throw open the window and stick my head outside and scream silently into the ether, the void, the nothingness.

This is the main evidence that I've lost my mind. I want to be there. In that nothingness. I wonder: Is it like in space movies and I would just float around forever? Or is it really nothing, like *BOOM!* I'm just gone? When I stick my head out the window in the middle of the night, the sky is black and endless and the stars are twinkling far away and maybe there's a moon or some drifty clouds. Beautiful. If my bedroom wasn't on the ground floor, I would leap into . . . into it, whatever it is.

───※───

When you change into someone you don't even recognize, it is not a good idea to start a new school. But my school, my sweet, safe Montessori school, only went up to eighth grade. I started going there when I was three and I never wanted to leave. I know all about dinosaurs and astronomy and how to use a kiln and grow kale and tomatoes and morning glories because of that school. Actually, it is called the Morning Glory Montessori School because the woman who started it back in the '70s was named Gloria and when she died, the teachers planted morning glories in her honor and changed the name from the Maple Street Montessori School to the Morning Glory Montessori School. We learned how to plant them and how to help them climb a terrace. They open in the morning, that's how they got their name. The flowers actually only live a day; they fade away a few hours before sunset. Luckily, the vines keep blooming until the first frost. Until then, hummingbirds and bees and butterflies come and drink from the flowers, and every morning in autumn we used to stand quietly outside and observe them.

My new school is not quiet in the morning, or ever. It's big and noisy and chaotic, with kids racing around with enormous backpacks on their backs like some kind of mutant turtles and bells ringing and scratchy announcements that no one can understand coming through the intercoms. I feel like a tiny speck of nothing trapped in a crowded hallway that smells like spilled milk and Axe deodorant and dirty gym clothes and bad pizza and a little bit of ammonia. I hold my breath as I let myself get pushed to wherever I need to go, just moving with the jostling from the crowd until I see my classroom, at which point I have to fight my way out of the throng.

I try to think about the morning glories, their vivid pink and blue in a dewy morning light. I try to think about my old school, which was in a red brick mansion that a rich family donated back in the 1970s because Gloria helped their children become creative, thoughtful citizens. That's what the plaque in the front hallway says. This school is old and brick, too, but not in a beautiful, magnificent way. Every hallway is painted a different, too-bright color— orange, purple, yellow, green—with lockers painted the same color along the cinder-block walls. The effect is like you've fallen into a giant vat of paint, and all I can think of is how in *Charlie and the Chocolate Factory* Augustus Gloop fell into that chocolate river and got sucked into the extraction pipe. My locker is in the orange hallway, and every morning as I struggle with the lock to open it, I think at any minute I could fall into the worst shade of orange you have ever seen and an orange river would lead me to a pipe and that would be that.

Somehow, maybe because I don't rush or push but just get carried along by other people's power, I am always the last one to class. I open the classroom door and step inside, trying to go unnoticed. But the teacher stops talking and the kids stop doing whatever they're doing and everyone looks at me slithering to my desk. The teacher might say, "Clementine, you need to try harder to get here on time," or some version of that. And I nod and mumble and take my seat at my weird plastic desk, which isn't a desk really but a chair with a foldable plastic tray that you can use when you have to write something or put your enormous textbook down.

Everyone gets back to learning or goofing off or whatever pretty quickly. But in that moment between when I walk in and when class resumes, I can hear exactly what they are all thinking as they turn to look at me. *She's the new girl. She's the one whose sister died. She's the one who tried to kill herself.* They are mostly right. I am new here. My sister did die. And six months ago, on an impossibly beautiful first day of spring, I swallowed most of a bottle of ibuprofen. I hear the words that are in their brains as if they are speaking them out loud. The teacher starts talking again, but I just sit there, listening to what they're thinking. *She's the one who has lost her mind.*

CHAPTER TWO

IN WHICH I HAPPILY SAY AGAIN, "YES, VIRGINIA, THERE IS A SANTA CLAUS"

FIRST WEEK OF OCTOBER

Mom says, "I have a great idea. Let's go visit Virginia and her family."

She says this because I am lying on the couch with exactly three pillows over my face. Actually, she says it because I've been lying here all day. I don't think she knows that I made sure there were three pillows. Or that I have the thumbs and pinkies of both my hands bent down, leaving exactly three fingers straight up. Or that lately I've been doing lots of things in threes. Like I tap the side of a door three times whenever I go into or leave a room. I take three sips in a row of whatever I'm drinking and three bites of whatever I'm eating without talking in between.

Mom knows me better than anybody else so she says the one thing that might actually get me off the couch: *Let's go visit Virginia.*

Virginia has been my best friend since before we were born—her mom and my mom met in their Lamaze breathing class when they were pregnant with us. Virginia and I had the good sense to be born a day apart so they were even in the hospital together, and they started a Mommy and Me class so, as they say, "we wouldn't go insane," and then we all started taking family camping trips on weekends and renting a little house near the beach for a couple weeks every summer. Even better: Our families used to line up perfectly. Mom, Dad, me, Halley. Mom, Dad, Virginia, Celeste. Virginia and me the same age, Halley and Celeste the same age.

Then a drunk driver going the wrong way on the highway plowed into the car our fathers were in and just like that, it was just our moms and us. I was only four when it happened so all I remember is playing with my Polly Pockets one minute and Mom screaming the next minute. I remember the house filling up with people and lots of crying and whispering. I remember Virginia and her family staying over for a long time and not going to pre-K and worrying I was going to miss the apple festival at school.

What I don't remember is my father, or the happy times we all spent together making s'mores and collecting seashells. We have so many pictures of us as a family that I almost feel like I *do* remember, but it's kind of like remembering a scene in a book instead of in real life. Virginia claims she has very sharp, vivid memories: her dad picking her up and spinning her, her dad reading to her and using different funny voices for the characters, how when her dad made homemade pizza he put her hands on the rolling pin and then his big hands over hers and they rolled the dough out like that. But my dad is just a blurry figure dressed in denim and plaid, floating through the rooms of our house. Halley was way too young to remember him, but she always said, "He smelled like rain."

To me, the air in our house changed in some significant but inexplicable way. It used to be like electricity and then it went kind of flat. Virginia and her family ate spaghetti at our house every Friday and had us over for tacos every

Sunday night, and we still all went camping and even to the beach for two weeks in the summer because our mothers believed we needed continuity. Our mothers drank too much chardonnay and got silly together, but always ended up crying in each other's arms. "Sorry, girls," Mom would say, "we're in our cups." Once, a couple of months after our fathers died, Virginia and I took a bottle of chardonnay into her room on Taco Sunday and drank the whole thing and threw up. The only good thing about it was our mothers decided we had a stomach flu and put us in Virginia's soft bed with ginger ale and cool cloths and a pot in case we needed to throw up again. I got to sleep over and skip school the next day and just stay in bed with Virginia watching reruns of *My Little Pony* and *Strawberry Shortcake*, our favorite shows back when we were kids.

Then, completely out of the blue, last year Virginia's mother announced that they were moving to Vermont. Vermont! A million miles away. No more Spaghetti Fridays or Taco Sundays. No more weekend camping trips or sleepovers. No more Virginia and Clementine. Even worse, Virginia's mother was getting married. I didn't even know she had a boyfriend. But apparently she had gone to her high-school reunion and ran into her old high-school boyfriend, who lived—big surprise—in Vermont, and they "picked up where they left off all those years ago," according to her. She announced all of this at our house over spaghetti and meatballs, her eyes shining and her cheeks pink. I guess Mom knew about the guy, which explained the frequency of weekend sleepovers at our house. Virginia and Celeste had met him a few times and everyone got along great. I wasn't able to swallow the big mouthful of meatball I had when this announcement was made, so I kind of pushed it over to the side so I could talk, and asked Virginia if that was true. She looked mostly confused, but she said, "I guess so," and her mother beamed at her. Just like that, they were gone.

When Mom suggests we visit them, I slide the pillows off my face and say, "In Vermont?"

"Yes, in Vermont. Where else would we visit them?" she says, slapping my arm playfully.

"Will the husband be there?"

"Jack. Of course he'll be there, Clementine," Mom says. "They're *married*."

"And Poppy will be there, too," I say, overstating the obvious yet again.

Poppy is the baby Virginia's mom and Jack had. A baby! Even saying Poppy's name is hard. Nothing makes sense anymore.

"Oh, Clementine," Mom says, "sometimes you wear me out with your questions, kiddo."

I worry that she might change her mind because I am just too difficult, so I say, "Of course I want to visit Virginia! Are you kidding?"

Mom grins. "Well good," she says. "I thought you might."

The whole way to Vermont I can't stop thinking how weird, how off-center everything is. It's just Mom and me in the car with our broken hearts, going to Vermont to see a family of five. Mom, me. Jack, Virginia's mom, Virginia, Celeste, Poppy. That was very unbalanced. Sometimes, like now, I feel a hole in the universe in the place where Halley is supposed to be. Like in Mom's old Passat wagon, I feel Halley's not-here-ness. There's a big Halley-sized hole. I reach my hand into the space between Mom and me, like I might actually find a part of Halley there. *He smelled like rain.* I keep my hand up, searching in that space, and think of Halley smells: strawberry shampoo, Mod Podge glue, nail polish.

"Clementine, what are you doing?" Mom says.

She's frowning. My hand is searching that spot.

"Nothing," I say. But I can't seem to stop my hand from moving like that.

She just shakes her head.

"Remember *Yes, Virginia, there is a Santa Claus*?" Mom asks after a while.

We have entered Vermont and right on cue there is foliage, the leaves shimmering yellow and red and orange at us. There is a sign for apple cider and another one for apple cider doughnuts. It's like we've driven into a postcard.

"Of course, I remember," I say. We pass some cows in a perfect green field with perfect golden haystacks. I decide I hate Vermont.

"You and Virginia were so little," Mom says, launching into the story. Even though I know it by heart, I love hearing her tell it. "What? Five or six? And for some reason, Virginia announced there was no Santa Claus, that he wasn't real, and you said—"

"I said, *Yes, Virginia, there is a Santa Claus*—"

"Even though you didn't know that was a thing, saying that, and Allison and I could not stop laughing, so you and Virginia and Celeste and Halley started laughing too because laughter is so—"

"Contagious," I finish because I look over and I see that Mom is crying.

The end of the story is that when our moms caught their breath, they told us how like a hundred years ago some kid named Virginia wrote in to the newspaper and asked if there was a Santa Claus, and the editor answered her right in the newspaper that there was. "How dreary would be the world if there were no Santa Claus," he said. "It would be as dreary as if there were no VIRGINIAS." Whenever Virginia asked an obvious question, everyone answered her with, "Yes, Virginia, there is a Santa Claus," and we would all burst out laughing.

Mom and I don't say much after that, partly because it takes her a while to stop crying and partly because she has to pay attention to the road, with all its twists and turns. I reach over and hold her hand, even though it's supposed to be on the steering wheel, and we sit like that for a long time.

I consider telling Mom that a part of me feels nervous about seeing Virginia because I haven't seen her in so long, except at Halley's funeral and that doesn't really count. When she moved, we promised to write each other *real* letters, but after just one exchange we didn't write any more. We didn't even email each other except a couple times. I think she doesn't know what to say to me about Halley or the ibuprofen or anything, and I don't know what to say to her about any of that, either.

Mom has stopped crying and I think maybe I can tell her how I'm feeling, but the navigation is saying, "You've arrived at your destination," and Mom mutters, "Finally," and we are pulling into the driveway of an old white farmhouse. Behind it, rolling hills stretch forever. There are big, old trees stretching their dazzling arms, and a curly-haired golden dog appears from nowhere, wagging its tail. Mom beeps the horn twice, her old signal announcing we were there, back when *there* was a yellow split ranch half a mile from our house.

The door flies open and people come running out. Celeste, two braids flying behind her. Virginia's mom, gently steering a red-haired toddler. Jack, and then Virginia. Everyone is rushing over to us except Virginia, who stands halfway between the door and me.

"Clementine?" she says. "Is that really you?"

"Yes, Virginia," I say, "there is a Santa Claus."

With that she whoops with laughter and races into my arms, falling on top of me onto the soft green buttercupped grass.

CHAPTER THREE

IN WHICH I LEARN TO HATE THE STATE OF VERMONT

Virginia's room has green-and-white wallpaper that looks like ivy climbing up it. She has a white iron bed with a hand-stitched quilt on it and there's a rocking chair that looks like it's about a million years old in one corner of the room with a hardcover book open and turned facedown on the seat. I kind of feel like I walked onto a movie set. SETTING: A VERMONT FARMHOUSE. I try to remember Virginia's old room that she shared with Celeste. IKEA twin beds. Beanbag chairs with their names on them. Two mismatched bureaus. Lots of junk and cat hair everywhere. I look around this room. Movie set, I think again.

"It looks like you live in *Little House on the Prairie*,"

I say, not knowing where to sit.

Virginia smiles like she's not sure if I was being nice or mean. (I admit it: I was being mean. And maybe a little jealous. Okay, maybe a lot jealous.)

"Except that was Kansas," she says, picking at a thread on the quilt.

"Thus the prairie part," I say.

Virginia pats the bed for me to come and sit beside her, and I do.

"Do you like it here?" I ask, mostly to break the silence.

Virginia smiles, a real one this time, and nods vigorously. "I love it! In the winter, we go skiing for phys ed."

"You ski?" I blurt. We are not skiing families. We are beach families. "I mean, skiing? Down mountains? Really?"

More nodding. "It is so much fun. You have to come when there's snow and we can go skiing. It's like flying," she adds softly.

"Wow," I say for lack of something better to say.

We sit awkwardly for a bit, me trying to picture Virginia in ski clothes like they wear in the Olympics and

Virginia thinking who knows what.

"Hey. Don't tell anyone," Virginia whispers, "but Mom is pregnant again. Isn't that exciting?"

"I guess?" But I'm thinking it is not exciting. It's just one more thing throwing off everything that used to be.

"No, no, it is. Really exciting," Virginia says. "You can't believe how great it is to be in a family."

"I am in a family," I say.

"I know," she says, "but I mean, like, a real family."

"Instead of just two people?" I say.

She looks horrified. She stammers and stumbles on apologies and corrections and I don't help her one bit.

"I guess I mean a family like the ones on television," she says finally.

"I have news for you," I say, getting off the bed and heading for the door. "Television isn't real, Virginia."

I have tears burning the backs of my eyes and an overwhelming urge to get out of that room and that house and just run and run. But run where? Through those fields? Back down the road? Home?

Just like that I'm down the steep, narrow stairs

and bursting out the front door into the blinding sunshine and too-blue sky. The dog sees me and jumps to his feet, ready for something.

I hear Mom calling me, her voice confused and surprised. But I keep running, opting for those fields. It's gotten colder and I can see my breath coming out in little puffs and hear myself panting, that's how hard I'm running. The dog has decided to follow me, and keeps up with me, right by my side.

Mom's voice is getting closer. I glance over my shoulder and see there's a whole parade of people following me: Mom, Virginia, her mom, Celeste. Being the youngest, Celeste is the fastest and she catches up to me first.

"Is it a race?" she asks, those dumb braids flying behind her again.

I glare at her and run faster.

Now Virginia has caught up with us and she's telling me she's sorry and I run harder so that I leave her behind, too.

"You have to catch her," Mom yells. "She might hurt herself!"

When I hear that, I stop, just like that.

I turn around and face all of them.

"I'm not going to hurt myself!" I scream.

They all stop, too, standing in front of me like a firing squad, staring.

I stare back.

The dog is rolling in the grass at my feet. He's the only one having fun so far. I drop to the grass and close my eyes and I roll, too. The grass is cold and a little wet and I smell things rotting.

"Clementine?" Mom says softly.

But I just keep rolling around like the dog, like a person who has lost herself completely.

—⋇—

No one makes any real eye contact with me over dinner, which is pumpkin soup served in actual pumpkins. There's a swirl of something white and roasted pumpkin seeds on top. Before dinner we all sat around eating Vermont cheddar cheese with Vermont apples. Now the Vermont pumpkins. Vermont is making me weary.

It's weird but even the baby, Poppy, doesn't look at me. I try to play peekaboo with her because every baby likes peekaboo, but the kid ignores me. She just giddily smashes her pureed pumpkin into the high-chair tray with her fists and throws applesauce on the floor. Virginia and her family are talking about how great the schools are here and how fun it is to ski and ice-skate in the winter and how tomorrow we will hike to Robert Frost's cabin. I want to put my head down on the table and sleep.

There's some strange spice in the soup and the musty smell of it makes me nauseous. I pick out the pumpkin seeds and chew on those.

Mom laughs nervously. "I hope you don't mind if I have another glass of chardonnay," she says as she pours.

Both Virginia's mother and Jack are drinking some Vermont-made seltzer water.

"Have you given up wine, too, Allison?" Mom asks. I'm not sure what else Virginia's mother has given up, except her entire old life.

"Well," Allison says slowly, and a shy smile creeps onto her face. "Actually." She glances at Jack, who beams back at her.

"Actually?" Mom says, her glass of wine midair on its way to her mouth.

"We're having a baby," Allison says.

She reaches across the table and squeezes Jack's hand and in that moment my nausea increases because I realize that they are making babies in this very house. *Doing it.* While Virginia and Celeste and Poppy sleep. I can taste that weird spice rising in my throat so I gulp some fresh Vermont milk—*From right down the road!*—to shove it back down.

"Wow," Mom says without any enthusiasm. "Another baby."

"Another girl," Allison says. She rolls her eyes like she's so disappointed by this but it's clear she's the happiest person in the world.

"Hey, why don't you two vote on the name?" Jack says. "We can't seem to find one we both like."

He gets up and retrieves a small notebook and a pencil. While he flips through the notebook to find whatever page he's looking for, I think about how Virginia and I used to laugh because we got the depressing names—Virginia, after Virginia Woolf, the writer who filled her pockets with stones and threw herself into a river; and Clementine because Dad loved the song "Oh, My Darling Clementine," even though she also drowned in a river—and our little sisters got the beautiful ones. Halley for a comet and Celeste, which means heavenly.

"Clementine?" Allison is saying. "Which do you like best?"

I glance around the table. Jack is holding the pencil, ready to take my vote. Mom has finished her wine and her face is starting to look blurry, the way it does after a few glasses of chardonnay.

"Please, please pick Daisy," Celeste says.

"I don't think she should have a flower name," Virginia says like she's said the same thing a million times. "Poppy has the flower name."

"How about Lizzie? Like Lizzie Borden," I say, trying to make a joke with Virginia. A woman who killed her parents with an axe! Another depressing name! But Virginia stares at me, horrified.

"Lizzie isn't on the list," Jack says. "We have Daisy, Olivia, Aura, and Ruth."

Mom pours herself more wine, splashing some on the oak table. "Ruth," she says. "I vote for Ruth. It sounds like an old lady's name."

Jack's jaw tightens, but he just says, "One vote for Ruth," and makes a scratch mark in his notebook.

"Say Daisy," Celeste stage-whispers to me.

Suddenly, after not looking at me for the entire dinner, they're all staring at me. Even the baby has her head cocked and her oversized blue eyes are staring right at me.

"Halley," I say. "Why don't you name her Halley?"

Mom makes a strangled noise, like a sob is trapped in her throat and wants out.

"Like the comet," I add, even though I know I'm being a jerk.

And then Mom does what I've been wanting to do. She puts her head right down on the table. But instead of going to sleep, she lets that sob out and a whole fountain of sobs follows.

CHAPTER FOUR

IN WHICH I STILL DON'T KNOW WHOSE WOODS THESE ARE

"You seem so different," Virginia said to me before we went to sleep last night.

She said it after she turned off the lights so I couldn't even see her face.

"Yeah, well, my life pretty much sucks," I said.

She didn't answer me and quickly pretended she was asleep.

But this morning she's acting all normal again. Maybe her mother gave her a talking to, like, *Be nice to Clementine. Her sister died and she's sad.*

We drive up a winding mountain road, then park the car and hike into the woods. Jack, who teaches literature at a college nearby, bores us with facts about Robert Frost.

The baby is in a complicated-looking backpack on Jack's back and even she goes to sleep. Did we know Robert Frost was actually a city person even though he is famous for writing about rural life? That he was nominated for the Nobel prize thirty-one times? That he read a poem at John F. Kennedy's inauguration?

"Interesting story," Jack says. "He wrote a poem called 'Dedication' specially for the inauguration but the glare from the sun was so strong he couldn't see the page."

I narrow my eyes to try to see if the cabin is up ahead. Nothing.

"So he recited 'The Gift Outright' from memory," Jack says.

"Wow!" Allison says. "From memory!"

"'The land was ours before we were the land's,'" Jack says, and Celeste gets all excited.

"Now *you're* reciting it from memory!"

"Jack knows every poem by heart," Virginia tells me.

I stop myself from saying, *Every poem? Really?*

"Say the duck one," Celeste pleads, tugging on his arm.

"'Behold the duck. It does not cluck,'" Jack begins, and just like that they are all saying the poem together, bursting out laughing when they reach the last line: "'It bottoms up'!"

Mom catches my eye, and that thing passes between us that people who are close can share with just a look. They are driving her bonkers, too. I smile and she rolls her eyes and we both feel better.

"I see the cabin!" Celeste says, and runs ahead.

"Frost lived and wrote here in the summer and fall," Jack tells Mom.

"His son died," Mom says flatly. "From cholera, I think. He was only four or five and it nearly destroyed Frost."

Jack clears his throat. "I'm sorry I never got to meet your daughter," he says softly. "I'm sorry for your loss."

"Thank you," Mom says. "Yes, everyone is very sorry."

I slip my hand in hers, something I haven't done since I was a little kid, but this is the second time in twenty-four hours. For some reason, I think about the night after Halley died and how I climbed in bed with Mom and the two of us held on to each other like we were the last people left on earth. We were. Without Halley, we were.

—⋇—

After dinner—*Lamb! From right down the road!*—Virginia asks me if I want to go for a walk. Since we hiked all day, I really don't want to go for a walk but I realize she's trying to be nice, so I say yes. Her mother lends me her fleece jacket because the weather has turned cold, and it's too big for me, but I feel cozy in it, my hands lost in the sleeves and the smell of apples floating up from it. The sky has more stars than I've ever seen, and I can't stop looking up. There's the Milky Way, clear as can be, and the Big Dipper.

"No light pollution," Virginia says, gazing up, too.

We are walking through the field behind her house. The cold air meets the warmer air and creates an eerie fog floating above the grass.

"I hope we don't run into any vampires," I say.

"Once I saw a bear right over there." Virginia points. "It was enormous."

"Great."

She laughs. "They only come out early in the morning or at dusk, according to Jack."

I almost say something about what a know-it-all Jack is but decide against it.

"We're almost there," Virginia says a little while later.

"We're actually going somewhere?"

"It's a little creepy, but I like it," she says.

We come to a crooked gate, and she opens it. It's like the fog is hugging our knees and everything feels damp and cold. Virginia has stopped walking.

"Some of these are over two hundred years old," she says.

That's when my eyes adjust and I can make sense of what I'm looking at: a cemetery. A really old cemetery. Most of the headstones are leaning or half buried, worn out from so many years out here.

"I love cemeteries," I say.

"Me too."

I think about Heron Hills, where Halley is now. That cemetery is beautiful, the headstones all gleaming gray or white or pink stone and marble, even the old ones.

"It's a family plot," Virginia explains. "That's how they used to do it. One family lived here, in the house, until the 1960s, then Jack bought it just a few years ago."

The moon casts enough light for me to see. A lot of the inscriptions have worn off, but I can make out some writing.

"Poor Elizabeth Alden," I say. " 'She suffered.' "

"This is my favorite. Mariette du Peaux. Only thirteen years old and from Paris, France. Why was she in Vermont? What happened to her?"

"Maybe she had a peanut allergy," I say.

It is so quiet here. I don't think I've ever been somewhere so quiet.

"Maybe," Virginia says into the silence.

"That day?" I say, my throat tight. "I went in the kitchen and made a peanut butter and jelly sandwich."

"Okay."

"What I don't know is if I washed the knife really good."

Virginia looks at me. "What are you saying?"

"If I didn't, and someone came in and used that knife for the bagels the kids at Halley's table were eating . . ."

I don't finish. I don't need to. I can tell Virginia gets what I'm saying by the horrified look on her face.

I watch her thinking, and then she nods and says, "You

did wash it really good. I know you did. We were always so careful, reading all the food labels and not swapping cookies or anything with anyone. Always."

She's right, of course.

Then she says, "I feel so bad that I wasn't in school when it happened. That I was so far away."

"I wish you were there, too, but I'm also glad you weren't because it was so terrible."

"Did you go in the ambulance with her?"

"Yeah, but they wouldn't let me sit with her. They said I had to sit in the front where there was a seat belt, but I could tell it was really bad. Different than the other times."

I think about how eerily quiet it was in that ambulance, except for one EMT barking orders at the other one. I kept saying, *You're going to be okay, Halley. We're almost there.*

"She probably died in the ambulance," I tell Virginia. "I mean, they kept doing things to her, even at the hospital, but I think she was already gone."

Virginia says, "Remember when our mothers made us all memorize 'Stopping by Woods on a Snowy Evening'—"

"Probably just to get us out of their hair—"

"And Halley kept having trouble learning it—"

"And she got so mad," I say, picturing her, only seven or eight years old, her face red with frustration.

"She said, 'Who the hell's woods are these, anyway?'"

Virginia and I both crack up.

When our laughter dies down, Virginia says, "Poor Halley. Poor you."

"I'm cold," I say because I kind of want to hold on to our laughter and the little bit of closeness with Virginia that I feel right now.

"Let's go back," Virginia says.

At the gate she turns and says, "Good night, sweet souls."

The fog has grown thicker and we have to hold on to each other's arms as we grope our way through it.

"Who the hell's woods are these, anyway?" I say to myself, but Virginia hears me and laughs.

I look up at the sky. So many stars.

CHAPTER FIVE

IN WHICH I BREAK OUT OF THE SNOW GLOBE

I don't want to go to school and tell Mom when she comes to get me out of bed on Monday morning.

"But I made pancakes," she says, as if that's a reason to do anything. "I wanted to use that Vermont maple syrup Allison sent us home with."

"From right down the road!" I growl, and place three pillows over my face.

"What?" Mom says. "Down the road?"

"Nothing."

"Well, come and get it while they're hot!"

Didn't she hear me say that I don't want to go to school today?

"Clementine, you are absolutely going to school.

Doctor Morgenstern says routine is essential."

"Doctor Morgenstern is *your* therapist," I remind her. "She's telling *you* that you need a routine."

"Everyone needs a routine," Mom insists. I can feel her looming over me, waiting.

"Fine," I say after counting to thirty-three in my head. I fling the pillows off my face and the covers off the rest of me.

"Did you sleep in your clothes?" Mom asks, disgusted.

"So what?"

She stares at me, her lips moving slightly as if she's trying out answers. Obviously, she can't find any, so she just walks out. I follow close behind, but she spins around and says, "Well change into something fresh! You can't go to school in clothes that you slept in!"

I don't see why I can't do that. No one talks to me or looks at me except when they whisper about me, and that's usually behind my back. I could wear just my underwear and no one would notice. But I do what Mom says because I'm exhausted by this conversation. I open drawers and stare into my closet and move clothes around, trying to find something that will make me blend into the background, kind of the way the maps and grammar tips and posters teachers hang on the walls blend in. You know they're there, but don't pay any attention to them.

Finally, I put on Halley's rust-colored sweater that she hated and traded with me for a baby-blue one that I hated and I brush my hair enough to get the biggest tangles out. By the time I get downstairs, the pancakes are cold and Mom is shoving them down the garbage disposal, crying.

"I like cold pancakes," I say.

"Just go to school, okay?"

The table is set for two with the bird plates I like— pale green ones with different birds on them, their names written in fancy scroll beneath. Hummingbird and Cardinal are out and there's maple syrup in the gravy boat. The sight of it all breaks my heart. I wonder how many pieces a heart can break into? The garbage disposal roars and Mom keeps it going, even after it has stopped chewing up the pancakes.

First period. Algebra. I'm late as usual so by the time I walk in there are already kids at the board doing equations in colored chalk. The teacher, Mrs. B, has an intricate system that involves using different colors for different functions. I didn't pay attention when she explained it, and since I don't do my algebra homework, I never go up to the board. I slither to my seat and the two girls who sit across from me roll their eyes at each other. They are best friends and oddly their names rhyme. Lacy and Casey. I don't know which is which.

My seat in this class is by the window, the only good thing about algebra. I look out at the world, feeling like I'm in a snow globe. I'm stuck in here, and the real world is out there. I can see cars driving past and the tops of buildings. If I squint, I can make out some of the tallest buildings downtown: a gold domed bank and the steeple of a church.

"Pssst," I hear, and swing my head slowly toward the sound.

It's Lacy or Casey, leaning slightly across the aisle between us.

Mrs. B is at the board, erasing parts of the equations with her sleeve.

"Hey," the girl whispers, "is it true you tried to kill yourself? Like for real?"

"Do you have scars or anything?" the other one asks.

"Oh," I say, "I have scars. Deep ones."

I'm speaking metaphorically but I've still got that image of my heart crumbling, breaking into ever smaller pieces.

"Can you . . ." Lacy or Casey lifts the cuff of her own sweater, which is soft gray and looks like a cat's fur. "You know, so we can see?"

"My scars are here," I tell her, and I tap my chest.

They look at each other and try not to laugh.

"My heart isn't whole anymore," I explain. "It's broken up into millions of pieces, tiny pebbles that rattle around in there."

One of them giggles.

"What a freak," the other one says.

"Can you hear them rattling around in there?" I ask them, and I get out of my seat and stand close to them. "Can you hear them now?"

They look at each other again.

"Miss Marsh?" Mrs. B is saying. "Why are you out of your seat?"

"Because I have to do something," I tell her.

"Do you need a hall pass?" she says. Her left sleeve is completely covered in pink and blue and yellow chalk dust from erasing the board with it.

"No, thank you," I say.

Everyone is looking at me, of course.

You know how when you shake a snow globe, snow or sparkles fall gently? That's what I feel, like I'm shaking and something is falling over me.

"Do you want to go to the nurse?" Mrs. B asks, and a low titter spreads through the class.

"Sit back down now please," Mrs. B says.

I look down at Lacy and Casey, who are smirking, and I want to wipe those smirks off their lip-glossed lips, so I grab one of them by her furry sweater and with my other hand I start slapping her face. Not hard. Just small slaps around her mouth.

Kids gasp and I hear someone say, "Mrs. B? Do something?"

I can't stop and now she gets hysterical and the other one pushes me hard enough that not only do I let go but I fall backward, right onto the floor.

"You freak!" the one who pushed me yells.

Mrs. B is standing over me and I can see that she's shaking and not sure what to do, even though she can see

I'm okay because I'm getting up. She reaches an arm out, maybe to help me, but I shake her off and start to gather my things.

Mrs. B says very firmly, "Miss Marsh, go to the office. Now."

"You should call the police!" the one I slapped says. She's got her hand to her mouth and fat tears are rolling down her face.

"You need to go to the nurse," Mrs. B tells her.

"I'll take her," the other one says, and they walk out, arms draped around each other.

Everyone watches them go and then everyone looks back at me.

"Okay now," Mrs. B says as she walks back down the aisle to the front of the class, her eyes boring into me. "Enough drama for today."

I leave, but I don't go to the office. Instead, I walk right out of the school and all the way home, where I make microwave popcorn and watch the Weather Channel because there's something comforting about the dark red swath over California and the rain in the Midwest and the swirl of storms out at sea.

CHAPTER SIX

IN WHICH I RETURN TO CITY OF ANGELS

I am sure the school called Mom and reported that A: I slapped another kid, and B: I walked out during first period. But for some reason she doesn't say anything. I think she doesn't know what to say anymore. I keep doing weirder and weirder things and she probably is just trying to figure out what to do next for me.

Mom is surprised when I tell her I want to go the City of Angels meeting.

"I thought you said it was pathetic to keep going there," she reminds me, which frankly I don't need my own words thrown back in my face, thank you very much.

"Well," I say, "maybe I'm pathetic then."

"No, no! I'm glad you want to go. I think it helped

you process things," Mom says carefully.

City of Angels is a grief group for kids who have lost siblings. It is the most depressing place in the world, but at least being around other people who have experienced what you've experienced keeps you from feeling like a freak (to quote Lacy and Casey). Plus Gloria, the woman who runs the meetings, is the coolest person in the world. Maybe there's something about the name Gloria that makes someone glorious? A Gloria started my Montessori school and a Gloria runs meetings for broken kids.

The reason I said it was pathetic to keep going to those meetings is that the longer you attend them, the clearer it is that you are not moving forward. It's the kind of thing you do at first, when you can't think straight and your whole world is different and you think you're the only person who feels like this, who has ever felt like this. City of Angels shows you that you aren't alone. And that there's a way out. Look at Gloria, so wise and cool and smart and funny. Her sister died but here she is, normal. Better than normal. Someday, I used to think, I will be a Gloria, too. But then months and months passed, and the kids who were there with me at the start stopped coming, and before too long everyone was new. Except me. The one who not only wasn't any better but was actually worse. (As demonstrated by intentionally overdosing on Advil.)

By now, even the former new kids from City of Angels would be gone, so maybe I won't seem as pathetic as I am. Only Gloria will know.

Mom is putting the pork chops she was going to make for dinner back in the fridge because there's pizza at City of Angels. She bustles around, putting a cardigan over her shirt and locating her shoes. Once she has her handbag slung over her shoulder and the car keys in her hand, I put on my jacket and try to make nice.

"Thanks for taking me," I say.

"Clementine," Mom says, and I see that her bottom lip is quivering, "I will do anything, absolutely anything, to help you. Do you know that?"

"I do," I say, though I hadn't considered this really.

"Anything," she says again, passionately this time.

I feel like we are about to fend off Confederate soldiers or make our way to a covered wagon heading west. *Anything!*

﹉

As I suspected, I do not recognize one person at City of Angels. Everything is exactly the same—Dixie cups of tepid apple juice, chairs arranged in a circle, glassy-eyed parents with their glassy-eyed kids mill around or stand frozen in place—except all the players are new.

"Clementine!" I hear Gloria exclaim, and then she's hurrying toward me, and then she's giving me a hug.

"Wow," she says.

"I thought it would be nice . . . ," I begin, but Gloria cocks her head. There is nothing nice about this place.

"Helpful," I say. "To come."

"You're not doing so hot?" she says softly.

"If smacking a girl in the face, walking out of school, and binge-watching the Weather Channel means I'm not doing so hot, then yes, you're correct."

I forgot all about Mom, but luckily she's over by the coffee urn with most of the other parents.

"I'm glad you came," Gloria says.

She steers me toward the circle of chairs.

"It's a good group," she says. Then, soft again, "I'm happy you're here."

As the senior member of City of Angels, I used to be all showy. I shared everything. I was center stage, a symbol of teenage grief. I cried and shouted and said outrageous things on purpose. But tonight, I don't say anything at all. I just listen to kids talking about their sisters or brothers, about fate and karma, about the dangers of swimming pools and genetic diseases and off-balance big-screen TVs, about pain and numbness. As each person speaks, I tell myself that I'm not a freak.

"My name is Marisol and I can't sleep because why did God take my baby sister for no reason and all these other awful kids keep on living?"

I am not a freak.

"I don't believe in God," a kid named Petie says. "If there's a God, he wouldn't make me suffer like this."

I am not a freak.

"If I hadn't been in such a rush, Flora would have put on her helmet. This is all my fault," William says.

I am not a freak.

"I haven't said this out loud," Marilu whispers, "but I didn't even really like my sister very much. That makes me feel awful."

I perk up when Marilu says this.

"Do you want to say more about that?" Gloria asks gently.

Marilu looks at her, terrified. "I don't think so?"

"Hey," Gloria says, "this is something a lot of us feel. When someone dies, they're often mythologized. All their bad traits vanish and they become the most wonderful, perfect—"

"Angelic," a boy volunteers, which makes some kids giggle.

"Yes! Angelic," Gloria says. "How many of your parents have actually started collecting stuff with angels on it?"

Hands shoot up.

"My guess, Marilu, is that you loved your sister *and* she made you mad," Gloria says.

Marilu shrugs. "Maybe, but mostly I just didn't like her. She was a cheerleader and talked about boys and makeup and clothes and stuff. She was, I don't know, frivolous."

"Tell you what," Gloria says, "let's go around the circle and say one thing we hated about our sibling and one thing we loved. Okay?"

Gloria starts. "My sister was a tattletale. It drove me wild. Minor infractions. Major infractions. All reported directly to our mother."

There's some laughter and heads nodding.

"But I loved how at night she would put her cold feet between my knees to warm them up, and then we'd switch, and I'd put my cold feet between her knees."

Gloria passes around the misshapen rag doll—it's supposed to be an angel but bears no resemblance to any angel I've seen—and as each person takes it they share a bad thing and a good thing.

I want to listen. I do. But instead I work hard, really hard, at shoving down this scary feeling rising up from my guts. I don't want a turn. I don't want to do this. I start to sweat. The angel is two kids away from me. The boy holding it is crying as he speaks but I can't focus on what words are coming out of his mouth. Then the boy right next to me has the angel, and I'm sweating even more and my ears are ringing and then the angel is in my hands.

I do my breathing, in and out, in and out. The ringing fades. My sweat turns cold.

"I can't think of anything," I croak.

Gloria leans forward in her chair.

"Anything bad? Or . . ."

"Right," I say quickly. "I can't think of anything bad about Halley."

What I don't say is that really, lately, I can only think of bad things about Halley, about how she used to bother me and make me mad. It's kind of like after I told Virginia about the peanut butter on the knife, I opened this whole other dark place: I don't like Halley.

Gloria studies my face, then says, "Okay. Not even something like she mixed all her food together when she ate? Or she cried too easily?"

I shake my head.

"Okay," Gloria says again.

After the meeting, I tell Mom I don't want to stay for pizza. When she presses me about wanting to leave, I make up a big project that's due tomorrow.

"I want to get a good grade," I say, because she is worried about my terrible grades from last year and I know she won't argue with this reasoning. Besides, I can't tell her the truth, that I want to avoid Gloria. And myself.

On the way home, Mom surprises me by going to the McDonald's drive-through. She boycotts McDonald's because she and my dad had decided that their kids wouldn't ever eat fast food and would have healthy meals instead. Since he died, she's given up on those ideas mostly. But for some reason, she holds on to the McDonald's thing. So, this is a real treat.

I order the Chicken McNuggets Happy Meal, six pieces, and extra nuggets on the side, and dig in as soon as Mom hands me the warm box.

"Want a fry?" I ask, dangling one at her.

She starts to shake her head, then laughs. "Why not?" she says, and I pop it in her mouth.

To my surprise, the toy inside is a Buzz Lightyear figure. I was expecting Thor or some other Marvel character. But it's Buzz, Halley's favorite *Toy Story* character staring back at me. I shove it back in the box so Mom doesn't see. It would make her sad, like it's making me sad.

"Clementine?" Mom says after she steals a couple more fries. "The school called today. Mr. Lombardo?"

I don't look at her. I just keep eating my McNuggets, keeping a tally in my head as I do. I eat them three in a row, then stop, then three more. So far, I've eaten six. I wonder if threes make me feel safe because we used to be a family of three.

"He said you slapped somebody?"

"Uh-huh."

"Why in the world would you hit someone? Ever since he called I've been trying to think of why you would do that. And what I should say to you about it."

"She made me mad," I say quietly.

"Okay," Mom says. "And you felt out of control or . . ."

It comes back to me, that smug look and her lip-glossed lips and the sarcasm.

"She thinks I'm a freak. Everyone does," I say.

"Oh, sweetie," Mom says, like her heart is breaking. "No."

"They do. Because I guess I am a freak. They're right."

Almost like I'm proving it, I pop three more McNuggets in my mouth, one after the other, and think *nine*.

"Here's what I need to you to do," Mom says. "I need you to go to school tomorrow and try, *try*, to make one friend. Just one. Someone who sees you for you, not for all the things that have happened to you. Can you do that?"

"I don't know."

"You can, Clementine! I know you can."

"Okay."

"And tonight," she says, "you have to write a letter of apology to this girl. Lacy? And to the algebra teacher. And, sorry, but you also have detention all week."

I know that she has negotiated this stuff with Mr. Lombardo, so I have to do it, even though I am not at all sorry.

"Thanks," I manage.

"You really want to thank me? Then you'll give me some more fries."

"They're good, right?" I say, passing the box over to her.

When we get home, I turn on my desk lamp so she can see light spilling out beneath my door and think I'm actually working on my fake big project or writing those apology letters. But what I'm really doing is lying on my bed with my clothes still on, staring up at the ceiling, trying not to think.

CHAPTER SEVEN

IN WHICH I EXPLAIN WHY I AM NOT ON THE PROVERBIAL COUCH

I should have a therapist. Maybe even a psychologist. And a psychopharmacologist. Or maybe all three. Because then I would get *help*. I would *do better*. I wouldn't have such dark thoughts. Or insomnia. Or act so inappropriately. I would be *normal*. Maybe even join clubs and go watch basketball games and have kids to my house for sleepovers. I would be a typical teenager instead of who I am.

But I've tried therapy. I spent almost a year with Doctor Debra Applebaum, a woman with pale blond hair and small blue eyes and round pink cheeks that looked like . . . well . . . apples. Sometimes she wore narrow, rectangular glasses the same color as her eyes. Sometimes she wore her hair in a messy bun. She always wore pastel-colored blouses or sweaters, a sea of sherbet greens and oranges and pinks. She always wore clogs, with thick striped tights if it was cold. She always had an amber-colored glass bowl of Hershey's Kisses on the table between us, and I never knew if I should take one to be polite, or if my taking or not taking one was a sign of something. But there they always were in their shiny foil. In other words, Doctor Debra Applebaum was predictable.

Her predictability felt like a challenge. Like I needed to shake her up somehow. So some days I wouldn't talk for the whole fifty minutes. Some days I wouldn't stop talking. Once, I took my shoes off, just to see what she would do. But there was no shaking up Doctor Debra Applebaum. No matter what I did or didn't do, she just sat patiently in her tangerine-orange chair and made notes with an old-fashioned number two pencil, the kind you need a pencil sharpener to sharpen. I looked for a pencil sharpener somewhere in that office, but never found one. Did she use a knife? Her teeth? I mean, the pencils were always perfectly sharp. But how?

Doctor Applebaum's technique was to ask me benign

questions. "How was that math test?" Or, "Are you still watching *Survivor*?" Somehow my answers were supposed to open the door to *bigger things*. But they never did. Doctor Applebaum sat in her tangerine-orange chair with her clogs and her number two pencils, and I sat across from her on the green settee (her word, not mine), and the Hershey's Kisses sat in a glass bowl on the table between us. Week after week.

After I took too many Advils, I briefly saw Doctor Jeremiah Lange. He chewed on an unlit pipe during our fifty minutes. I think he colored his hair to hide the gray. He wore scuffed-up loafers and colorful argyle socks and saggy jeans. No matter what I said, he said, "Uh-huh," and made a note on his iPad. I started to think he wasn't actually making notes, that he was playing Words with Friends or online poker instead. After a while, he told my mother we didn't click, and he referred us to Doctor Sylvia Lewandowski.

Doctor Lewandowski was from Warsaw and she had a thick, lovely accent. She ate hard-boiled eggs during our fifty minutes, and she wore slip-on bedroom slippers with off-gray pantyhose. I told my mother Doctor Lewandowski and I didn't click. Also, the smell of hard-boiled eggs made me gag. It took my mother a month or so to find a new doctor, and this one was the worst of all.

Doctor Carrie Grey looked like she was just a couple years older than me. She had a sparkling nose-ring stud in one nostril and an intricate tattoo sleeve of something I couldn't make out but that looked very jungle-y. Parrots maybe. And jaguars. And lots of vines. She insisted I call her Carrie, not Doctor Grey. She wore Birkenstocks, no socks, and her hair always looked uncombed and twice she apologized but said she was too high to talk today. "Let's just sit here and close our eyes, okay?" she said. "Let's just, you know, be." I didn't close my eyes. I watched her sit there with a dopey grin on her face and her head moving to music only she could hear. "Carrie," I said after fifty minutes, "I'm going now." "Cool," she said. After the second time that happened, I told my mother that Carrie and I were not clicking. Besides, even when she wasn't high, she spent most of the time telling me *her* problems: bad boyfriend, had to move again, fight with her mother. "Honestly, Clementine, I don't know where else to go," Mom replied. "I thought Doctor Grey was a good fit. She's young and she's, I don't know, cool."

I had one session with an ancient doctor who told my mother I was more than she could handle at this point in her career.

I had one session with a nice, round-faced woman who called before our second session and said she had to cancel because she was going on maternity leave.

I had one session with a distracted guy and another with an angry guy.

Mom wanted me to find a doctor more than I did. These fifty-minute sessions, though interesting for all the wrong reasons, did not make me feel better. At all.

I did leave Strawberry Fields after my Advil overdose with prescriptions for antianxiety pills and antidepressants, but they made me feel like I had cotton in my head. Also, they made me very thirsty and my lips smacked loudly whenever I talked and everyone stared at me, probably wondering why I didn't drink more water.

"Okay!" Mom said enthusiastically one night at dinner right before I started my new school. "I found someone who I think is perfect. Doctor Pamela Pointer. Her specialty is kids just like you, Clementine."

I wondered what that meant. *Kids just like me*. With

dead sisters? Or dead fathers? Or both? Who overdosed on Advil? Who heard sounds in the night? Who felt like a robot, or anesthetized, or like an anesthetized robot?

I chewed my mac and cheese and waited.

"She's so popular that she has a waiting list!" Mom said, like that was a good thing, which actually for me it was because I didn't want to see Doctor Pamela Pointer or anyone else.

"You have an appointment right before Christmas," Mom said, sliding an appointment card across the table.

The card was hot pink.

"She has a website!" Mom said, like this was the most amazing thing ever.

The website was on the hot-pink card, www.ihearyou .com.

As soon as dinner was over, I went to the computer and typed in www.ihearyou.com. A picture of Doctor Pamela Pointer on a windswept beach popped up. Her long hair was blowing in the breeze. She was barefoot and wearing white pants with the cuffs rolled up and a blue linen shirt, sleeves also rolled up and only the middle two buttons buttoned. She was looking off in the distance, thoughtful. It looked like a magazine ad for tampons.

The word WELCOME was at the top, and when I clicked it, a new page opened.

I was a girl like you once. Dreamy. Misunderstood. Sad. Confused. Angry. I made mistakes. Lots of them. I was lost, for a long time. Then, I had an epiphany, and I knew my calling was to help others like me. To help them avoid the mistakes I made. To help them right themselves if they did make those mistakes. I have dedicated myself to self-improvement. I am a certified yogi and Shiatsu massage therapist. I seek wisdom from the sea, from the tarot, from the magic of stones and crystals. I share all of my wisdom with you as you walk your path.

I hear you.

Pam

"Have you looked at that website?" I asked Mom later that night. She was watching *Masterpiece Theatre* and I knew she didn't want to be interrupted, even though

Helen Mirren always solved the crime eventually.

"Website?" Mom said, eyes on Helen.

"ihearyou.com."

"What are you talking about?"

"Doctor Pamela Pointer, yogi and massage therapist and tarot card reader?"

Finally, she looked at me. "I know she's kind of out there, Clementine, but at this point we're kind of desperate, aren't we, kiddo?"

It broke my heart that Mom said *we're kind of desperate*. Why was Mom desperate?

I was the desperate one, wasn't I?

"Maybe I do need my tarot cards read," I said, which made Mom smile, which made me smile.

"You never know," Mom said.

I pointed at the television. "What I do know is that Helen Mirren will definitely solve this crime."

"Want to sit with me and find out?"

I didn't really, but then I thought of *we're kind of desperate* and I said, "Sure," and curled up on the couch, actually hoping the yogi/massage therapist/tarot card reader could help me.

CHAPTER EIGHT

IN WHICH I BECOME A PURITAN

There's a kid in my English class named Miles Pierce who keeps glancing over at me and when I stare back at them, they blush and look away. Typically, classmates don't like me. I'm too outspoken, bad at small talk, and overly emotional. And that was *before* Halley died. Now I'm too outspoken, bad at small talk, overly emotional, and I have a dead sister and I tried to overdose on Advil. So. Yeah.

But Miles Pierce. They're the only kid in class who chose *they/them* pronouns. I'm not sure what that means about them, except that they're brave to do that in a school with so many jocks and shallow people. Miles is shorter than me. Their bangs kind of swoop across their forehead in a way that reminds me of the way boys in British boarding schools wear their hair in movies. Their hair is dark blond and their eyes, from sitting three rows behind them diagonally, appear to be of the gray variety. They have nice, straight teeth, like they just got their braces off over the summer, and they wear untucked shirts over jeans. They are, overall, unremarkable looking.

But still, maybe a classmate liking me will lift my spirits and take my mind off how depressing my life is. How depressing everything is, actually. Also, it's been one week since I promised my mother I would try to make one friend, and I haven't done that yet. Miles seems like a good possibility. So when our teacher, Ms. Quigley, announces we are going to work in groups and to gather with four other students to form a group, I make my way over to Miles and kind of hover, indicating I'm in their group now. Samantha, the spacey girl who sits next to them, does the same thing, so now we are a group of three.

"Jayden, go join the group with Miles and Samantha," Ms. Quigley says.

"And me," I tell her.

"And Clementine," she says, making a note on her iPad.

I guess Miles didn't see me hovering because when Ms. Quigley says that, they turn around and immediately blush. I smile at them, hoping my smile looks normal and not maniacal. Smiling has started to be difficult. Sometimes when I smile, I feel like I'm baring my teeth, like I'm about to attack. Other times smiling hurts my mouth. It's like I'm stretching my lips into an unnatural shape.

"What's this group for?" Samantha says as if she just woke up.

"Something about *The Crucible*," Jayden says.

Samantha looks confused. "What's that?"

"The play we've been reading for like a month," he says.

Ms. Quigley is telling us to be quiet and settle down. She always wears sweatshirts with sayings on them, kind of like my mom's pillows. Today's says: *Sorry! Did I roll my eyes out loud?*

"Each group will do a presentation on a specific

question about *The Crucible*," she says. "But before I give you your topic, I want you to come up with a name for your group. Be creative!"

"I hate doing things like this," Jayden mutters.

Jayden is a scholar athlete, which this school makes a big deal about. Scholar athletes have their pictures hanging in the main lobby and whenever their names are mentioned, it's always with *scholar athlete* in front of them. So Jayden is always *Scholar Athlete Jayden Vargas*. To be a scholar athlete, you have to play at least two sports and have a ninety or higher grade point average. Needless to say, I will never be a scholar athlete.

"How about the Puritans?" Miles suggests.

"Nah, everybody's going to pick that," Jayden says dismissively. He already looks bored.

"How about the Scholar Athletes?" I say.

He doesn't look bored now. He looks mad. "Funny," he says. "How about the Freaks?"

Samantha checks back in. "I like that!"

Miles seems embarrassed. "I . . . I don't think that's a good idea."

"I like the Puritans," I say.

"It's dumb," Jayden says. "And obvious."

"Is it true that scholar athletes always get into Ivy League colleges?" I ask him.

"The Ivies?" Samantha offers. "Or something like that?"

"Yeah," Jayden says, narrowing his eyes at me. "So?"

I shrug. "Just wondering."

We all just sit there after that and don't say anything. When we have to announce our group name, Miles tells Ms. Quigley, "The Puritans," and she pops her eyes and writes it on her iPad. No one else picked that name, which I point out just to bug Jayden. Then we get our topic: The Crucible *as an allegory about the anti-communist frenzy of the McCarthy period.*

"Like Paul McCartney?" Samantha says, confused.

I look at Miles and say directly to them, "I'm psyched. I love communism."

They panic. "Um," they say. "Um."

"I don't love communism," I say quickly. "I mean, I love talking about it. In history, in its historical context, I mean." I'm smiling and I'm certain it's the baring teeth kind, because Miles seems terrified.

"It's such an obvious topic," Jayden says. "Obviously

Miller meant it as an allegory for just that."

"Miller?" Samantha says. I notice the more confused she becomes the wider her eyes get. They're like flying saucers now. "Miller who?"

Miles has calmed down a bit. "I think it's an interesting topic, too, Clementine."

I check to see if I feel anything different or special, but I feel as flat as ever.

"You know that movie, *The Day the Earth Stood Still*? Not the 2008 remake, but the original one?" I say just to Miles.

I don't wait for them to answer. "That was an allegory for the Cold War."

"Really?" they say, impressed, which is what I was hoping for.

"We are a movie-watching family," I say. "That's a classic for us. Maybe we can connect it somehow?"

"I like that idea," Samantha says. "We could go to the movies together and watch it?"

"Well, it's old," I tell her.

"We could watch it on Netflix," Miles offers. "At my house."

"I think we should stay on task," Jayden says. *"The Crucible* as an allegory for communism. No sci-fi movies with Keanu Reeves—"

"He was in the remake," I tell him.

"—or Cold War stuff—"

"That *is* communism," I point out.

He puffs out his cheeks, then sucks them in. Like I do when I breathe to calm down.

"I hate this group," he says, more to himself than to us.

He stares across the room longingly to where scholar athlete Star Plimpton, scholar athlete Brett Barrett, and scholar athlete Manda Newhouse sit looking serious. Somehow they managed to form a group together before Ms. Quigley could send them off into groups with mere mortals. One unlucky girl is also a Moonlight Dancer (their group's name) and she is staring off at nothing while they plan and organize and make outlines.

I look right at Miles and say, "I like this group."

"Me too," they say, and blush.

"Me too!" Samantha says with too much enthusiasm.

Jayden groans, and Miles and I make eye contact that

says how much we think he's ridiculous and how funny Samantha is and about a million other things. The eyes are the windows to the soul, Shakespeare said. Or something like that. I look away because I don't want Miles to see that deep into me. It's way too scary there.

CHAPTER NINE

IN WHICH I KISS A BOY

"Can you drive me to this kid's house?" I ask Mom, trying to sound nonchalant like I do this normal thing—going to someone's house—every day. "We're doing a group project on *The Crucible*."

"Wait. What? A kid's house?" Mom says, grinning. "Like a friend's house?"

"I told you I'd make a friend," I say. What I don't tell her is that my apology letters were pretty lame.

Dear Lacy, I apologize. Clementine.

Dear Mrs. B, I apologize. Clementine.

"And what is your friend's name?"

"Miles."

"Miles," she says. "Good."

"Yeah, so *Miles* is showing our group *The Day the Earth Stood Still* on their, like, million-inch big-screen television," I say.

Mom is now searching in her purse, or whatever you call the giant bag that she carries around. It's a weird shade of yellow, not quite Dijon and not quite baby poop, and it's big enough to hold her knitting project and a rain hat (because you never know when it might rain!) and even a regular-size purse inside. This bag is like one of those Russian nesting dolls, I think as I watch her pulling things from it. In a way, I realize, everything is like one of those Russian nesting dolls. Even people. Inside the big one there are tons of other ones, seemingly identical yet different in some small way.

"Found them!" Mom says, waving the car keys in my face. "So where does this Miles live?"

I recite the address and she lets out a low whistle. "Fancy neighborhood," she says.

When I get in the car, I tell her, "It was my idea to

watch the movie since it's also an allegory for communism."

"Brilliant, kiddo. But I kind of wish you were reading something less depressing than *The Crucible*. Like *Inherit the Wind*. That's a good, non-depressing play."

I don't know that play so I just say, "Okay."

"Or *My Sister Eileen*. That's a fun one. My high-school theater group put that one on."

The whole way to Miles's house she talks about the plot of *My Sister Eileen* and how the woman who wrote it was writing about herself and *her* sister Eileen, and on and on and on. Finally, we are pulling up in front of Miles's McMansion.

"Wow," Mom says, staring up at the six chimneys. For some reason, the way she says this makes me think she likes it. A lot.

As soon as I get out of the car, the front door opens and there stands Miles, looking as ordinary as ever.

They wave to my mother and she sticks her head out the window and says, "Miles! Hi! I'm Clementine's mom."

I want to die of embarrassment because of course that's who she is and also, why doesn't she just drive away?

"Hi!" Miles says to her, and they wave again and she waves back and I'm about to scream but Mom does, thankfully, leave.

"Hi," Miles says, stepping aside to let me in. "She's nice."

"I guess."

"Everyone is already here. You're last."

"Sorry."

"No problem," Miles says, and starts to walk through the massive entryway.

I follow them into a soaring foyer and down some steps and through rooms of indeterminate usages until we are finally in what looks like a den from a Pottery Barn catalog, everything in subtle colors matching everything else and seashells in an enormous glass bowl and throw pillows that do not say weird things, or anything at all.

Jayden already looks bored, texting on his phone. He's wearing those weird long, baggy shorts that jocks wear and a sweatshirt with a number on it and white socks, no shoes. Samantha beams up at me with her big, empty eyes and says, "There's LaCroix!" She holds up a green-and-silver can for proof.

"So yeah," Miles says. "LaCroix or Poland Spring if you don't like bubbles. I do. Like bubbles," they add. "And there's pizza, veggie, plain, and pepperoni. And Caesar salad. You know, snacks."

In my house this is called a meal, but whatever. I take a grapefruit LaCroix, some pepperoni pizza, and Caesar salad, and sit in one of the comfy chairs.

"This is so fun," Samantha says.

"Jayden? Are you ready?" Miles says, pointing the remote at him.

"This is such a waste of my time," Jayden says, reluctantly putting his phone down and covering his face in his hands.

"Do you have a headache?" Samantha asks him.

"Yeah," Jayden says, "it's called the Puritans."

Samantha frowns. "Like our group?"

Thankfully, Miles starts the movie and we all go silent, except for chewing and opening more cans of LaCroix. I notice that Miles sits in the comfy chair right next to me and gives me a little smile when they do. I smile back. It feels like a normal one, but who knows? Luckily the room is dark so it doesn't really matter. At one point they put their arm on the armrest of their chair, and my arm is on my armrest, and I can feel the hairs on their arm and the heat from their skin. This should do something to me—excite me or repulse me or make me dizzy—but instead I'm like a scientist recording events. Hair on arm. Heat from flesh. Smell of green pepper from somewhere . . . their breath, maybe?

After a little while, they move their arm closer and now it's flat out touching my arm, the back of their hand against my wrist, which is kind of weird. I move my arm closer, too, so that our skin is pushed together. It's not unpleasant, but I mean, it's just arms. Mine is starting to feel like it's not even part of my body, like it's an independent thing. Miles scooches their hand so it's near my hand instead of near my wrist. And we watch the rest of the movie in this unnatural way.

"Thank God that's over," Jayden says as soon as the movie's finished.

Miles has walked over to a complicated box on the wall and the track lighting comes on low.

"I thought it was beautiful," Samantha says, and she sounds like she's crying a little. "The way the aliens leave and teach Earth that war is not the answer. I wish those aliens would go to, I don't know, places where there's war now and teach them that lesson."

"Where's the john?" Jayden asks.

Miles gives him a complicated set of directions and then, guessing they probably have a dozen bathrooms, I ask them where another one is. I want to find some toothpaste and scrub my teeth and tongue with my finger to get the pepperoni out of there in case Miles stands close to me or something. They tell me where to go but once I leave the room, I don't remember a word they said, so I just wander through all the rooms, trying to figure out what they're used for. Oddly, there's a sign on a door that says Pierce's Pub and another one that says Judy's Wine Cellar. Eventually, I find a bathroom. Everything in it is black and white, even the soap. In a black-and-white cup there's anise-flavored toothpaste that smells like Twizzlers and I rub it around my teeth and along my tongue. It doesn't make the pepperoni taste go away exactly. It just adds to the flavor.

Back outside, I wander some more, nothing and everything looking vaguely familiar. How does Miles's family find one another? I wonder, and just like that I turn a corner and bump into someone.

Jayden.

"Lost too?" he says.

"No," I say.

"Look what I found," he says, and holds up a bottle of whiskey. "This stuff costs like a hundred dollars a bottle and they've got six of them."

"You can't have that."

He raises one eyebrow. Smarmy. "I can't?" he says. He unscrews the top and takes a swig. "It tastes like a fireplace," he says, his face twisting unpleasantly.

Jayden holds the bottle out to me and I take a big gulp of it because why not? Maybe it will make me happy? Or silly? But it's so gross that I kind of choke on it and a spray of whiskey spews from my mouth.

Jayden laughs, but for once not unkindly. "You've got . . . ," he says, and wipes my chin with his fingers.

I yank my head back.

"Can I ask you something?" he says.

"No."

"I'm not trying to be a jerk here. I really want to know."

I glare at him.

"Did you see a white light? Or any dead people you know, like, coming for you?"

"Shut up," I spit at him. I turn to stomp away, but he grabs my shoulders and turns me back around.

"I really want to know," he says. "My mom died when I was in kindergarten and I always wonder what *happened*, you know."

"Your mother did not die," I say. "I've seen your mother."

"That's my stepmother. Nancy. She's been around longer than my real mother, but . . ."

"Oh. Well, I didn't take enough pills to see any white lights or anything."

He nods. He's still holding my shoulders and he does the strangest thing. He pulls me in closer and leans down and kisses me, right on the lips. I mean, a boy is kissing me. A popular boy. A scholar athlete. He has a scratchy chin. Slightly chapped lips coated with some kind of mint lip balm. The cold tip of a nose. I open my mouth a little and just like that his tongue drops in and moves around. All I can think is how weird I must taste and how cold his tongue is and kind of big. I poke it with my tongue, and he pokes back.

This is kissing? I almost laugh.

"Man," Jayden says softly after the kiss ends, which seems to take forever. "Who knew you could kiss like that?"

"Well, I can," I say. "Kiss like that."

"You taste like Twizzlers," Jayden says to my back as I walk away.

This time when I run into someone, it's Miles.

"I got lost," I say.

They nod. "Figured."

We grin at each other, or rather they grin at me and I grin back.

"You have such pretty hair," they say.

I know that I have kissed the wrong person, that Miles is sweet and not a scholar athlete and actually likes me. I should feel bad about this.

But instead, I just say, "I'm going to call my mom to come pick me up."

CHAPTER TEN

IN WHICH THE SECOND WEIRDEST KID IN SCHOOL TRIES TO BE MY FRIEND

The school cafeteria drama is real, not something made up by bad teen shows. Kids sit in clusters of other kids like them, whispering about the other clusters of kids. If you don't belong anywhere, walking through the tables with your pathetic plastic tray with its pathetic food feels humiliating. Sure, there are pairs of kids sitting together doing AP Calc or planning D&D sessions. And there are singletons, like me, forced to sit at the far end of a table of friends or alone at an empty table. I'm not sure which is worse.

Today I opt for sitting alone at one of the empty tables at the edge of the cafeteria. There are four of them, and three already have a sole kid sitting at them. I need to snag the fourth one, so I hold on tight to my tray, the smell of hot dog strong even though I don't have a hot dog, and make my way through the noisy crowd. I wonder if Miles has lunch this period, at the ridiculous time of 11:10 a.m., which could actually be considered breakfast. I wonder where they sit. Probably not alone in no-man's-land.

I look around, like maybe I can spot them and if I do, maybe sit with an actual nice person. But instead of Miles, I see Jayden staring at me from his table of scholar athletes. He's staring at me like he didn't have his fat, cold tongue in my mouth last night. He's kind of grimacing, and I see him elbow Star from our English class and then she's also staring at me. Star says something to the girl on the other side of her and they kind of laugh, more like a guffaw, I decide.

I narrow my eyes and stare back at Jayden, which requires me to stop walking but I don't even care. All the scholar athletes are looking at me now and all of a sudden I feel like I might cry. I try to take my deep breaths but can't because I'm holding in tears. I try to think of something snappy or witty to say, maybe something about scholar athletes, but my mind is like a white tunnel, like a piece of copy paper, like nothing at all.

Before I can stop myself, I stare even harder at Jayden and I open my mouth and I flick my tongue out and slowly run it around my lips, from the corner across my top lip to the other corner and across my bottom lip. *Stop!* somewhere deep inside me is screaming, but I can't. Star has her hands to her face in shock or disgust and the girl next to her looks terrified.

"What are you doing?" Jayden says, and I can see the words coming out of his mouth and they are in all capital letters. WHAT. ARE. YOU. DOING?

The table erupts in laughter.

The hot-dog smell and the humiliation make me want to throw up, and I try to decide if that would make things a little better or whole lot worse. I land on worse, so I swallow back the metallic taste rising in my throat and start walking again to that table, their laughter hitting my back and head like pellets of ice.

Of course, my delay means that another loner has snagged the table, so I sit down at it, anyway, but at the seat farthest from her. My grilled cheese already has gone hard and cold and I can see a layer of grease shining on top of it. The fries are undercooked, too white, also hard, but I douse them with ketchup and eat them, anyway.

"Hi. I'm Agnes."

I look up and find that the kid at the other end of the table has slid over so that she is sitting directly across from me. Agnes. Her hair looks like she chopped it herself with pruning shears. It's dyed jet-black and tipped with violet, which wouldn't be too weird if her eyes weren't exactly like that, too: violet eyes surrounded by thick jet-black eyeliner. The effect is unnerving.

"I want to be in a punk rock band," she says. "Or become a marine biologist. Or a professional ice-skater."

I chew my saturated fry and try to think of a response.

"But I don't play any instruments," she continues, "except my brother gave me a ukulele and I read somewhere that it's really easy to teach yourself to play the ukulele, like on YouTube. Do you?"

"Do I?"

"Play any instruments?"

I shake my head. I think of the long-ago recorder lessons Halley and I took at Morning Glory, and the thought makes my heart stop pounding because I can practically feel the late afternoon sunshine that came in the window and smell the cookies the music teacher always made for us—Scottish shortbread, buttery and salty.

"Well, recorder," I say. Mine was apple green and Halley's was goldenrod yellow.

"I want to learn how to skate," Agnes says as if I hadn't said anything, "so I can be in the Ice Capades. Or maybe Disney on Ice." She sighs. "I love Disney. Can you name all the princesses? I'll give you a hint: There are twelve. I'll give you another hint: Anna and Elsa don't count because Elsa is a queen in *Frozen* and Anna is a queen in *Frozen II*. Okay, go."

"Cinderella?" I guess.

Agnes beams. "Yes!"

"And the one from *Beauty and the Beast*?"

"Belle. I'll give it to you."

"And maybe Pocahontas?" I say, wondering why I was even doing this. Was I this desperate to talk to another human being? Was Agnes going to be my second new friend? "I guess Jasmine is a princess."

"You have four!" Agnes says.

Can there really be eight more? Then I remember how Halley loved *The Little Mermaid* and we had to watch it over and over, even though I didn't like it at all, so I say, "Ariel."

Then my mind goes blank again and I'm sitting in our living room on my turquoise beanbag chair with my name on it in orange and I'm yelling at Halley that *I will not watch this stupid movie again! I hate it! I hate you!*

"Do you want another clue?" Agnes is asking. "Think Scotland."

I squeeze my eyes shut and with them still closed I say, "I was thinking about Scottish shortbread just a minute ago."

"Merida," she says, not sounding enthusiastic anymore. "From *Brave*."

I open my eyes. "I never saw that one."

"Well, I bet you saw *Snow White*, didn't you?"

The cafeteria is starting to clear out, even though the bell hasn't rung yet, because kids like to go to the vending machines and get candy bars or chips and stand around together in the same cluster they just sat in together and try to look cool.

"And you saw *Sleeping Beauty*, didn't you?"

Agnes sounds like she's getting angry and since she is one of the kids who eats alone, I don't know what she's capable of doing. I mean, I've been known to slap people. Like maybe she'll turn the table over or something, so I say, "Right, right, Snow White and Sleeping Beauty—"

"Aurora," Agnes says. "She has a name, you know."

I watch the scholar athlete table of kids get up all together, like they've practiced rising at the exact same time. Synchronized standing. I try to make one of them fall through mental telepathy. While Agnes is berating me for forgetting Mulan—"The second princess to wear pants!"—and Moana—"The other princess to have her name in the title!"—I am sending bad thoughts to the scholar athletes. *Fall! Fall!* But they glide across the cafeteria with perfect posture and grace.

Defeated, I look back at Agnes, who is glaring at me.

"There are only two more," she says.

I stand and pick up my tray. "I give up," I say.

"Pathetic," she mutters.

The bell rings, but Agnes just sits there. "Rapunzel? Tiana?"

"I've never heard of Tiana."

"The only princess with dimples?" Agnes says, exasperated.

I shrug and start to walk away.

"Want to sit with me again tomorrow?" she asks. Her eyes look sad and wet, hopeless. That's better than my flat ones.

"Okay," I say, even though Agnes is maybe the strangest person I've ever met and she kind of scares me.

"Really?" she says, jumping to her feet.

I nod. "Sure."

She throws her arms around me awkwardly. "You'll eat lunch with the second-weirdest kid in the school?" she says. Her breath smells like dimes.

"Yes," I say, hoping that no one sees us in this embrace.

"You know who the *weirdest* kid in the school is?" Agnes whispers.

If she's only the second weirdest, I can't imagine who is first, so I shake my head.

She has me practically in a headlock now and she holds on tighter.

"You!" she says, and releases me with a push before laughing and walking away, leaving me standing alone in the empty cafeteria.

CHAPTER ELEVEN

⋇

IN WHICH I TAKE TO MY BED

NOVEMBER

At three in the morning, I wake up because I hear a sound. Footsteps maybe, or rain. I look out the window and there is no rain, just darkness and moonlight from a gibbous moon. There are thin clouds, too, that look like someone finger-painted them up there. I remember that song my mother used to sing to Halley and me at bedtime—*Rows and rows of angel hair . . .* That's what these clouds look like. Then I remember that Mom had that song played at Halley's memorial service and how it made everyone bawl at the line, *Well something's lost but something's gained in living every day.*

My fingers jiggle the lock on the window. I could open this window and I could lean out into the dark night under the gibbous moon and people could spend the rest of their lives wondering if I fell or if I jumped. But then I hear the sound again. Footsteps. Down the hall. I stop jiggling the lock so I can hear better. It's 3:24 a. m. Mom is definitely not walking around. She's in her Ambien-induced sleep, which Doctor Morgenstern prescribed after Halley died. I saw on a television special report that some people have a reaction to Ambien and they do things while they're sleeping, like eat a pound of raw hamburger meat or paint their kitchen or even murder someone and they don't remember it at all the next day. When Mom suggested I take Ambien, I flatly refused. Just my luck, I would be a person who had that reaction.

Weird, but the footsteps don't sound like they're actually going anywhere, just kind of walking back and forth in the same basic area. Our house is small. Like maybe three or even four of our houses could fit inside Miles's. That means the hallway is short, with Mom's room at one end, my room on one side, the bathroom across from me, and Halley's at the other end. We used to have nubby gray carpeting on the hall, but one of Mom's projects was to pull it up and polish the scuffed-up floor beneath it. I think she'd hoped she would discover something beautiful under there, but it's obvious the rug was put down to hide the messed-up floor.

I slowly walk to my bedroom door and crack the door open.

"Hello?" I say into the dimly lit hall. Mom has a plug-in nightlight near the bathroom, but otherwise it's dark out there.

The footsteps stop.

I peek out enough to see that Mom's door is closed and her room is dark behind it. Same with Halley's. That door is hardly ever open anymore, although I know that Mom goes in there sometimes.

"If you want to sit in Halley's room," she told me once, "don't tamper with anything, okay, Clementine?"

"Tamper?" I repeated, because I only think of that word from cop shows—*Someone has tampered with the evidence.*

That sent me straight in there to see what there was to tamper with. But all I saw was Halley's room, just like she left it that day she went to school and never came home. The bed neither made nor unmade—she just pulled the blankets up without actually making the bed—clothes on the floor, art stuff everywhere, closet door open. Just a room. Nothing to tamper with.

"Hello?" I say again, and maybe because I was just thinking about Halley's untamperable room, I say it in that direction.

And there's a creak, like someone stepping on a floorboard.

I wait.

Nothing.

I keep waiting. More nothing.

I don't know how long I stand there like that, but when I get back in bed the sky outside my window has lightened. I can still see the moon, but the sky itself has changed from inky to navy.

I can only think two things: Did I hear a ghost? And, since I don't believe in ghosts, what does it mean that I think I heard one?

Okay. Three things. What does it mean that I think I heard Halley?

It can only mean I'm losing touch with reality even more. I tap the wall three times, like that will help somehow. But it doesn't. I still feel scared of ghosts and my own imagination.

Maybe I fall asleep because the next thing I know, Mom is standing over me, looking confused.

"Clementine? School?"

I shake my head and mumble something.

"Are you sick?" Mom says.

"Mom, someone was in the house last night. I heard footsteps."

"Oh, sweetie," she says. "That's just the house settling."

"I don't think so," I say, and my voice is kind of trembly.

"Houses make sounds, Clementine," she says. "They do."

"Well, I couldn't sleep."

She strokes my hair and I can practically hear her wondering what to do. To my great surprise, she says, "Okay, stay home today and rest."

I don't even pause to wonder why she's letting me skip school. I just slip back into beautiful emptiness.

—⫯—

Apparently, I was a fussy baby who never slept at night. I did enjoy sleeping during the day however. My grandmother—Mom's mom, we called her Gooey because that's how adorable baby me said Grandma—said that I needed to be turned upside down over a fire to fix my sleeping problem. So one day Gooey picked me up, turned on the stove, and carefully did a 360 over the flame with me. "And that's how I fixed *that* problem," she liked to tell us. Gooey was from a town in Ireland called Dingle, which made Halley and me practically pee our pants with laughter because, I mean, Dingle. "Go ahead, girlies," Gooey used to say, "laugh away. But I dare you to stroll along Inch Beach and not become smitten with Dingle. In fact, when you're teenagers I will personally send you both to Dingle so you can see for yourselves and that's how I will fix *that* problem."

Unfortunately, Halley never got to be a teenager and even if she had, Gooey died a few years before she did. "The cancer," Gooey had whispered to me from her hospital bed. A problem not even Gooey could fix.

She also couldn't turn me upside down over a flame again, so I stayed up all night jiggling the lock on the window and listening for footsteps and slept a deep, deep sleep all day. For three whole days I stayed up all night and slept when I was supposed to be in school, where Agnes sat alone at lunch thinking about Disney princesses and the scholar athletes accomplished things.

I was able to do this because Mom got a new job, working part-time at Forget-Me-Knot, the craft store in town. This job, which was basically being a salesperson, thrilled her beyond reason. All she did was ring up sales, restock shelves with yarn and fabric, and find the right-size needles or best hat patterns for customers. For her trouble, she got a 20 percent discount and came home every day with bags of yarn and buttons and needles. I was happy she was getting out of the house and talking to people and even about that discount.

Plus, the job allowed me to sleep all day and be left alone doing it. True, my nights were hell, spent in a paralysis of fear and thoughts of tumbling into the dark night sky. But then one day I opened my eyes just as evening fell and there was Mom, sitting beside me on the bed, watching me.

"That kid Miles has called you about a thousand times," she said. "About the project for English?"

In that moment I could not even bring to mind Miles's bland, ordinary face.

"I know you haven't been going to school this week. They have this robot call and report absences."

"Why didn't you make me go?" I wonder out loud.

"I don't know," Mom says, shaking her head. "I really have no idea. I purposely signed up for mother's hours so I would be at work while you were at school," she says, more to herself than to me.

I wonder what *mother's hours* means, but she keeps talking.

"I don't even know what I was thinking," she says, and just like that she has her hands over her face and she's crying.

"I didn't think!" she says finally. "It was a relief not to worry over you for a while. A relief," she says, the last *relief* coming out in a sobby voice that makes it about five syllables long.

"Oh, Clementine, I'm trying so hard to be happy, or something like happy. Optimistic, maybe? Something other than so, so sad. But how can I when I worry about you all the time? I'm so worried about you, sweetie. And so scared."

Even though I just slept for like ten hours, I want to curl right back up and sleep some more.

But I can't, because Mom has started to cry even harder, a big body-shaking cry that sounds like she's being strangled.

"I should have made you come downstairs to dinner," she's saying between sobs. "But I didn't want to. I wanted to just be myself in a room without a kid on the verge of doing something dangerous. Without having to watch everything you do, or try to read your expressions, or worry because you don't have any expressions and your face and eyes . . ." She paused for a second. "They're so flat. I just wanted to eat a pork chop in peace."

"Then it's working out," I say. "You can eat your pork chops in peace and I can stay in bed and sleep."

"No!" she wails. "No, Clementine. You need to sleep at night and go to school during the day and eat three meals every day. This is most definitely *not* working out."

It is for me, I think. But I know better than to say anything.

"Now you will get up and you will come downstairs, and you will eat this beautiful salmon I made. I marinated it in teriyaki sauce and I made rice and green beans and you will eat every bite."

I'm too tired to argue. The thought of a piece of teriyaki salmon turns my stomach. It was Halley who loved teriyaki salmon, not me. The teriyaki sauce does not hide the fishy taste of the salmon, in my opinion. Has Mom forgotten this? Or has she stopped caring what I like? Not that I blame her. I'm difficult and impossible and depressed and an overall killjoy. I am preventing her from being happy or optimistic or anything good. So I will just follow her downstairs and eat the disgusting salmon.

But as I sit across from her at the table, looking at that pale pink fish dyed brown on top on my plate, I realize that this is futile. Eating this salmon is not going to make her happy because nothing can make either one of us happy. We are locked in this other snow globe: two sad people at a small table staring at a piece of sad fish. When you shake this snow globe, I think, instead of snow or glitter, tears will fall on this scene. Gallons of tears. So many that the image of us at the table will be obscured, as if we have disappeared into our grief.

CHAPTER TWELVE

IN WHICH I AM SENT AWAY

The next day, I am deciding whether or not I can manage to go to school, leaning very heavily on I can't, when Mom calls me downstairs. It takes every bit of energy I have to do that, and when I show up in the living room she points to the recliner, a chair where Halley and I spent many hours playing with the lever that raises and lowers the footrest. It's a comfy chair, faded plaid, beautiful in all its ugliness. But the way Mom points and says, "Sit down, Clementine," it looks more like an executioner's chair.

I sit.

My feet keep pressing that footrest lever ever so slightly and my finger keeps tapping the button on the armrest.

Mom says, "I don't know what to do anymore, I mean with you not going to school and sleeping all the time . . ."

I can see she's upset, but all I can do is focus on *not* playing with the chair.

"And all I do is worry about you, sweetie. Worry when you're at school that kids are being mean to you. Worry because you're so sad. Because we're both so sad. Worry when you're by yourself that you might do something."

I hate to see her like this, her face all scrunched up and her hands twisting the hem of her shirt. Knowing it's all my fault only makes me feel worse. She's talking about experts, people equipped to help with what's wrong. She's talking about other kids going through stuff, how it helps to know you're not alone. I nod and nod and nod, maybe even mumble "I understand" a couple times.

Then Mom says, "You'll be home by Thanksgiving."

Suddenly, I'm not playing with the chair. And I'm not nodding.

"What?"

Mom has been pacing in front of me as she talks but now, she drops onto the couch like a person in an old movie fainting.

"You said you understand," she says.

"I said that because I wanted you to feel better."

"Sweetie, the only thing that is going to make me feel better is for you to get better. And this place, Sandy Point, I really believe they can help you."

"How? How can they help?"

"They'll get you in a positive routine. They'll help you be part of a community. You'll go hiking and swimming and there's group therapy and—"

My heart is racing the way it does when I'm scared. I've been in a psych ward and in a residential program at Strawberry Fields, but this kind of place is scarier somehow. This is the kind of place where really troubled kids are sent. But then I think that I am a really troubled kid.

"Here, see for yourself," Mom says, and hands me a brochure.

On the front of the brochure is a picture of four teenagers—white, Black, Asian, and Latinx—wearing enormous backpacks and looking weirdly cheerful that they are climbing a very steep, very rocky path. *Sandy Point: Where You Discover You.* Inside there are more pictures: kids by a bonfire, kids doing some kind of outdoor circle thing, kids looking intense as they climb ropes or kayak or sit alone on a big rock and think as the sun sets.

"I'm not going here," I say. "I hate things like rock climbing. I hate groups. You know that."

"All I know is we have to do something. And this looks nice—"

I glance at the brochure again, at those fake smiles. "Nice?"

"It's only eighteen days."

"But it's a place for . . . troubled kids. Messed-up kids."

Mom sighs. "We leave in the morning." She comes over and wraps her arms around me. "Kids like you," she says softly.

We arrive at Sandy Point a few minutes before noon, as instructed. The list of instructions is five pages long and includes the gear we needed to go to REI and max out Mom's credit card to buy. I googled Sandy Point last night and basically it's like Outward Bound for people who don't have any money. A low-rent Outward Bound.

There's a cabin surrounded by trees and the air smells like salt and pine, which would be nice if it wasn't here. As we walk toward the entrance, fallen pine needles crunch under my new ugly waterproof shoes. *Good for moderate climbs, kayaking and canoeing, walks and moderate hikes.* The only ones in my size were bright purple, so these shoes are the ugliest of the ugly.

Inside there's lots of activity. To the right, a dining hall where kids are busy doing things: setting the long tables, filling the salad bar, even working back in the kitchen. In fact, I don't see one adult in there. To the left there's a craft room. That one's empty. In the center, where Mom and I are standing, is a desk with a strawberry-blonde woman sitting at it, smiling.

"You must be Clementine!" she trills. "And Mrs. Marsh!"

Mom looks relieved. Maybe, like me, she's been worried this was going to be like those places we've seen in movies where kids are tortured or worked to death. There's so much light here, streaming in through the big windows and the skylight at the top of the soaring ceiling, as if they are telling us that only good things happen at Sandy Point.

"And you've got all your gear!" the woman says, indicating my new yellow duffel bag with her chin. "So now there's just the paperwork for you, Mrs. Marsh, and getting you settled into your room, Clementine, so you can make it to lunch by 1300."

She presses a button that doesn't make a sound we can hear, and a girl appears. She's around my age but looks exhausted and haggard.

"This is your roommate, Maeve. She will take you to your room."

And just like that, Maeve, who looks like she doesn't weigh even a hundred pounds, hoists my duffel bag and my new enormous backpack and starts off toward a wide-open staircase.

"Go on," Mom whispers to me. "It's going to be okay. She looks nice."

I hesitate.

"It's going to be more than okay," Mom says. "You'll see."

For a moment, I scope out escape routes. I could leave through the door we just came in. Or maybe out through the empty craft room. I don't want to stay here with Maeve and my gear and this smiling woman. I want to go home with Mom and get in my bed. But that's why I'm standing here now, isn't it?

Even the air in the room seems to be waiting for me to go with Maeve, so I just do. I stumble in my new ugly waterproof purple shoes, but I catch myself and just keep walking.

"Welcome to hell," Maeve says before she puts my stuff down. "Thirty days here can seem like forever."

I study this person who I'm supposed to live with for a month. Her once-dyed pink hair has dark roots that meet the pink just below the crown. Her eyebrows are all sparse and patchy, like they're trying to grow in. She looks like an untended garden.

"Bed linens are in here, clothes go in here, toiletries in here," Maeve is saying as she opens closets and drawers and cupboards. "You have to make the bed up yourself, this isn't a hotel, you know," she says in a falsetto, quoting someone. "And it must be made every day," she continues, still in falsetto, "and hair must be washed daily because you are here to learn *self-care* from the outside in."

She looks at me with her tired eyes. "It's all bloody nonsense," she says.

I nod. "Sure," I say.

I'm eager to make up the bed and climb into it, but while I'm stretching the fitted sheet around the corners, Maeve is telling me my schedule. Morning hike. Healthy breakfast. Group. Yoga. Journaling. Lunch. Group. Afternoon hike. Private session. Outdoor activity. Dinner. Debrief. Evening activity. Lights out.

I'm exhausted just listening.

"Then there's your duties. Kitchen. Cleanup. Vacuuming. Office work. Hike leader. Your duties change every week."

I realize I should have gotten myself out of bed and just gone to school, which would have been a lot easier than this.

In a low voice, Maeve adds, "I'll tell you who to watch out for. This place is full of tattletales. Also, I can point you toward who has contraband."

I nod again. "I guess I'll go say goodbye to my mother," I tell her.

"She's long gone. They aren't allowed to hang around."

"But we didn't say goodbye to each other."

Without waiting for her to reply, I hurry out of the room and make my way back to the lobby. It is still cast in lovely afternoon light that spills from the skylight and the big windows.

"Lunch is that way," the same woman at the desk says when she sees me.

"My mom—"

"Gone!" she says brightly. "You're all ours now."

Self-care, I learn pretty quickly, means tiring yourself out with hiking and climbing and cleaning and planting and baking and talking and creating things that are useless—plush fruit covered in colorful push pins, origami cranes, pot holders. There is always, always something that you have to do, no downtime, no relaxing, no television or books, except the one chosen by the Sandy Point librarian, Ms. Myrtle, that everyone has to read. Ms. Myrtle picks books that teach a moral lesson. My first week here the book is *To Kill a Mockingbird*, which I and everybody in the whole country has already read.

One evening during that first week, the evening activity is Letter Writing, led by Ms. Myrtle. We are handed stationery that looks like it's been donated by a Hallmark store—mine has a border of daisies around it, Maeve's has a cartoonish kitten in one corner—blue BIC pens, and a stamp. Our instructions are to write a nice letter to someone.

"Put the date at the top," Ms. Myrtle tells us. "Then choose a salutation. *Dear* is fine, but you can also use *Dearest,* or something of your choosing. Not *Hi* or *Hello,* which are fine in your text messages but not in your letters. Three paragraphs, followed by a sign-off. *Yours truly, Sincerely yours, Love.* Then sign your name."

Ms. Myrtle always looks surprised. Her eyeglasses, eyebrows, and bangs all point upward like tiny wings. I try to imagine her actually taking off, like Peter Pan and the Darling children. I imagine her dark-stockinged legs and weird lace-up shoes being airborne and laugh.

"We are writing letters now, Clementine," she says.

I stare down at my ugly paper with the daisies and chew the cap of my pen for a bit. Then I write:

Dearest Jude,

No, I'm not back in Strawberry Fields. I'm somewhere far worse. It's called Sandy Point, but there's no sand, just a totalitarian regime, too many activities, and bad food. (Are corn dogs actually food?) And what did I do to land myself here, you may be wondering? I slept too much!

Jude was my friend from City of Angels, younger than me but still someone I liked talking with, especially about Halley and his dead sister Katie. But after a while I stopped texting him back. I was only going to hurt him, and he deserved better than that. Better than me.

By the time Ms. Myrtle tells us to finish up, I've written him a very funny letter. I realize I'm not telling him the whole truth, just trying to make him laugh. It's less a letter to a friend and more a satirical essay. Or maybe, a small part of me thinks, it's an attempt to find the old me. The sarcastic, funny me. The me that once, in sixth grade, just for fun, dyed indigo streaks in my hair. Who played Little Red Riding Hood in the Morning Glory all-school production of *Into the Woods Junior* when I was only eight years old, beating out ten- and eleven-year-olds for the part. Who dressed up as the entire night sky for Halloween, a costume I thought up and made all by myself. Meanwhile, Halley wore a store-bought princess costume. Again.

> Dear Jude,
> I seem to be saying, can you see the real me in here?

We are told to address our letters—*be sure to put your return address!*—and stamp them and then hand them to Ms. Myrtle, who will mail them in the morning.

"I know most of you wrote to your parents," she says. "I hope you were honest. I hope you were real with them. You know?"

Some kids nod or look down at their feet. Maeve bites her cuticles.

What does it say about me, I wonder, that I wrote to a kid I used to know and practically nothing I wrote was exactly true? I try to think of what a letter to my mother would say.

Dear Mom.
I hate you for sending me here instead of letting me just sleep.
Yours truly,
Clementine

Dear Mom,
It's terrible here. Also, ridiculous. But I have a fake apple covered in bright red pushpins for your Christmas present.
Sincerely,
Clementine

Dear Mom,
Do you wish I had died instead of Halley?
Love,
Clementine

CHAPTER THIRTEEN

IN WHICH I PLAN MY ESCAPE

THIS IS WHAT SANDY POINT BELIEVES:

1. Routine is good for you.

2. Hard work is good for you.

3. Physical activity is good for you.

4. Community is good for you.

5. Art is good for you.

6. Reading is good for you.

7. Sharing your thoughts and feelings is good for you.

8. Household chores are good for you.

9. Fresh vegetables are good for you.

10. Believing you are valuable is good for you.

THIS IS WHAT I BELIEVE:

1. Sandy Point stinks and everything they think
    is good for you is a bunch of malarkey. Also: I
    am not valuable.

I volunteer for laundry duty because I like the smell
of clean clothes and the warmth from the dryer. Plus,
doing laundry makes me feel like I'm in prison, which I
basically am. The laundry room is in the basement but the
basement is not creepy. It's kind of modern looking, with
walls that are supposed to imitate Mondrian, an artist
I've never heard of before but who Ms. Myrtle thinks is
a genius. Why, I have no idea. His paintings are a bunch
of primary-colored squares and rectangles outlined in
black. That's it. I guess Ms. Myrtle painted the basement
walls, which have different-size squares in red and blue
and yellow.

At least it's brighter than most basements. Our
basement at home is unfinished. My father was in the
process of fixing it up when he got himself killed, so you
can see the beams and stuff that hold it together. The
floor is concrete, but someone—maybe Dad?—put some

gray indoor-outdoor carpeting on part of it. That's where we played Twister, because there wasn't enough room for all those arms and legs flying around in our living room.

The carpeting down here is the same color blue as the sky. Kind of pretty. The washing machines and dryers are in an alcove of their own, bright white and lined up against one wall like soldiers, ready to get to work. Against the other wall are all the sturdy canvas laundry bins and connecting the two walls is a long table for folding and sorting with a high red stool, which is where I sit and watch the clothes tumble around and around. I breathe that clean clothes smell and watch the clothes and my mind goes completely blank. It's like I'm hypnotized. When the washing machines ding to tell me they're done, I load the wet clothes into the dryers, hit START, and press my face against a dryer door, feeling its humming and its warmth.

Mom told me that when I was a baby and wouldn't sleep, she strapped me into my portable car seat, placed it on the dryer, and turned it on. All the shaking used to put me right to sleep apparently. So I have a long history with dryers. Maybe I should become a laundress. I've seen pictures in *National Geographic* or somewhere of women washing clothes on stones in a river. I could do that. I picture myself in a blue dress, barefoot, the sun beating down on me and I'm rubbing my shirts and stuff against smooth gray stones as water swirls around my ankles.

"What are you doing?" a voice interrupts.

I open my eyes and I feel the way it feels when I wake up from a dream, lightheaded and confused. There's a girl I don't recognize standing there, frowning.

"I mean, you have your face on the clothes dryer," she says. "And you're smiling."

She's holding a big straw basket of vegetables, which means she's on either garden or kitchen duty. There's a door in the basement that leads directly out to the yard. I notice her feet are dirty even though she's wearing the ugly dark green Crocs required as garden footwear. There are so many rules here I get weary just thinking about them.

"You're Clementine, right?" she says.

I nod. There's dirt under her fingernails, too.

"I'm Maggie. Maybe you've heard of me?"

I start to shake my head no but then I realize I have

heard of her. She's famous. Or infamous, actually. Rumor has it that Maggie has a stash of drugs that she sells, mostly pills, and also those little miniature bottles of liquor like they serve on airplanes. Apparently her mother is a flight attendant and always brings them home from her flights.

Maggie grins. Oddly, she kind of looks like a flight attendant herself with her tight blond ponytail and California-blue eyes, except she's so dirty.

"Ah! You have heard of me!" she says.

"Well," I say.

She waits, but that's all I say.

"Are you, like, high or something?" she asks, lowering her voice.

"What? No!"

"But you were *standing* there, practically *hugging* the dryer, and *grinning*."

"It's hard to explain," I say. "It relaxes me."

She looks skeptical, but shrugs and continues on her way back upstairs.

"If you ever want to *really* relax . . . ," she says over her shoulder, ". . . now you know who I am."

I watch her ponytail bounce as she walks away. Then I put my face back against the now very warm dryer and let it work its magic.

———⊰⊱———

All of a sudden, it's like Maggie is everywhere. I see her making a yellow pushpin banana in the art room and she's in my afternoon group session and she's on my morning hike and then she's on another morning hike, this one to some pond a million miles away. We're walking on pine needle–covered ground and I have purposely held back so I can be alone and not have to talk to anyone, but Maggie holds back, too, until I am walking next to her. She has that perfect ponytail and those big blue eyes and standing this close to her I realize she's super tall. I think of the Amazons from Greek mythology, a bunch of tall, fierce female warriors. At Morning Glory, we studied Greek mythology every year, always learning something new about the ancient Greeks.

I can still name all twelve Olympians, who are the major deities. I do it now, in my head, to help me ignore Maggie.

Zeus, Hera, Poseidon, Demeter, Athena, Apollo, Artemis, Ares, Hephaestus, Aphrodite, Hermes, and Dionysus.

"Um, hello?" she is saying, thrusting her face too close to my face. "I'm talking to you!"

I'm looking at her, right at her bright blue eyes and turned-up nose, but I'm thinking about how when Demeter's daughter, Persephone, went missing, Demeter ignored the harvest and wreaked havoc on the earth just to search for her. My mother just left me here. She wouldn't bargain with Hades to free me. She wouldn't even bargain with Ms. Myrtle.

Maggie takes me by the shoulders and holds on tight.

"Answer me!" she says, her cheeks flushing pink.

"Leave me alone," I say quietly.

I free myself from her grip and walk down the path. The others are way ahead of me, a colorful line zigzagging through the pine forest. I bet my mother would neglect the harvest to try and bring Halley back. She would go to the Underworld and negotiate for her return. She'd probably agree to having Halley with her for just two seasons, same as Demeter did, leaving her in cold, dark winter half the year.

—✸—

The pond is as gross as every pond I've ever had to swim in. Squishy bottom with reeds or something that get tangled around your legs. Murky water. The vague smell of rot. Because it's October, the water is freezing, but the sadists who run this place think cold water is good for you. They also think keeping windows open all the time promotes good health. Maeve told me that was a bunch of malarkey, that open-air schools were invented to stop the spread of tuberculosis. But everyone at Sandy Point believes that all this fresh air is going to make us better people, happier people.

By the time we jump in and out of that stagnant water, dry off and dress, sit on rocks to eat apple slices and orange wedges, and hike all the way back, I'm ready to drop. *That's why they do it*, Maeve told me. *They exhaust us so we can't think about whatever got us sent here.* Ha! I thought when she said that. Nothing can stop me from thinking about my sad, hopeless life. But of course we aren't allowed to nap. We have to journal about the activity and then start dinner chores. We have to go into the dining hall and eat our fresh vegetables and freshly baked bread and even more fruit.

I'm pushing my vegetable stir-fry around on my plate when who should come and sit across from me: Maggie.

"I picked those beans," she says, "so eat up."

The rice is brown and healthy, the vegetables are slick with soy sauce, and all I can think of is a greasy pepperoni pizza.

"With all your contraband," I say without looking up, "do you happen to have a pizza somewhere?"

Maggie leans forward, the tip of her ponytail dipping dangerously close to her stir-fry.

"That's what you want? A pizza?" she stage-whispers.

"Yup," I say, pushing my healthy dinner away from me. "Pepperoni."

"Come to my room after lights-out," she says. She gives me a grin that shows all her dazzling white teeth, then digs in to her food like it tastes delicious.

When she realizes that I'm watching her, she says through a mouthful of food, "I can't help myself. I'm from California. I grew up eating this stuff."

I have just one thought in my head: Can Maggie really get a pepperoni pizza tonight?

Because I am always so tired by the time the endless days here finally end, and because I love to sleep so much, I haven't ventured out of my room after lights-out. I half expect there to be guards positioned in the hallways, but the place is empty. Emergency lights glow eerily along the walls, but otherwise it's dark and hushed. Maggie's room is on another wing, so I have to walk through the main lobby, past the dining room, and down another hall. Everywhere I walk is still empty. I stop. How easy would it be to just walk out of here? I mean, there is no one around. The door where I walked in that first time is right there, waiting to let me out.

I glance around, half expecting Ms. Myrtle to step out of the shadows. But I'm alone. I walk on tiptoe to the door and take the handle in my hand, pausing to feel its coolness. Outside the big windows there're wisps of fog and the tall pine trees and moonlight. I lift the handle, holding my breath as I do. If this door opens, I am going to step outside into the chilly October night and walk all the way home. I glance down at my plaid flannel pajama pants and T-shirt that says *The Oxford Comma Preservation Society* and realize I might freeze to death out there. Virginia gave me this T-shirt after our sixth-grade teacher told each of us what punctuation mark we would be. Virginia was an exclamation point; I was an Oxford comma, the controversial, little-used punctuation mark that most people have never heard of.

My hand is still holding the door handle, like I'm afraid to lift it. Like it's better to stand here and think about punctuation marks. Just like that, I lift it and . . . nothing. It's locked. Of course. But an idea takes root in my brain. I could wear my fleece jacket. And socks. And I could pick this lock and escape. Note to self: Google how to pick a lock. I memorize how this particular lock looks so I can google the right thing, and then I walk down the corridor that leads to Maggie's room.

She opens the door before I even knock and pulls me inside.

"Can't dillydally," she says. "They'll see you."

I laugh. "That's what you think. There isn't a single person out there."

She laughs, too. "No kidding. They've got security cameras. Everywhere."

"Oh no," I say.

But she isn't listening. She takes a step backward and spreads out her arms. "Ta-da!" she says, and there before me, in all its greasy glory, is a pepperoni pizza, sitting in an open box, on her desk.

CHAPTER FOURTEEN

IN WHICH I PLAN MY ESCAPE, REDUX

It comes as no surprise to me that Maggie was sent here from her home in Santa Cruz, California, for continually breaking rules.

"Parents are divorced," Maggie tells me as we eat pizza. "Mom is a flight attendant who does San Francisco–Tokyo trips, which means she's gone more than half the month. Dad is an artist"—she puts air quotes around that—"who makes sculptures"—more air quotes—"out of salvageable material, also known as junk. Great role models, right?"

"Sure," I say.

Something is strange about her room, but I can't put my finger on it. I've only been in my own room and a few others on my hall—Nancy and Jessica's, Caroline and

Liza's—and that wasn't so much *inside* the room but more like standing in the doorway while they get their coats or whatever. That's when it hits me. I'm in a room with Maeve, Nancy is with Jessica, Caroline is with Liza, but Maggie seems to just be by herself. There's nothing on the other desk and the other bed is neat as can be.

"Who's your roommate?" I ask Maggie.

"Oh, she went home weeks ago and I never got a new one. Her name was *Faith*, because apparently her parents had a kid die and then they had her as a leap of faith. Creepy, right?"

I swallow hard at the part about a kid dying and can't seem to find my voice, so I shrug.

Maggie points a half-eaten piece of pizza at me and says, "What are you here for, anyway?"

I shrug again because I honestly don't know. "I guess because I wouldn't get out of bed."

"So depression?"

"Maybe?"

"I mean, if you tried to off yourself, you'd be on a psych ward, not at Camp Sandy Point."

There's that lump in my throat again.

Maggie frowns at me. "You need some water or something?" she asks, obviously noticing me trying to swallow. "Or maybe a long drink?"

She rummages around in a desk drawer and hands me a bright blue can (it kind of matches her eyes) with LONG DRINK written on it in white. Above it there's something about Finland and below it the year 1952. I open it and take a long swallow.

"That is disgusting," I say.

"Which part? The grapefruit? Or the gin?"

"Gin!"

Maggie laughs. "They all think it's seltzer. I drink it all the time, right in front of them."

I put the can down and get up to leave. But then I pause.

"So you really have all kinds of . . . stuff . . . here," I say.

"That's correct," Maggie says.

I think back to that afternoon last year when I stood in front of the open medicine cabinet and stared into it for a very long time, considering. The only razors were tropical-colored Daisy razors for women and those barely shaved my legs. Bubblegum-pink Pepto-Bismol. Antibacterial ointment and half-empty boxes of *Little Mermaid* and *Toy Story* Band-Aids. Nivea lotion. Sun Bum sunscreen. Q-tips. Antibiotic eye drops from when Halley got a paper cut in her eye. And: ibuprofen.

The bottle said not to take more than twelve in a twenty-four-hour period. So what would happen if I took, say, the whole bottle? I carried the bottle with me into the kitchen where I poured myself a big glass of orange juice in the to-go cup I got when the school went to see *Wicked*. It's got a green-faced Elphaba under a big black hat on it. Of course, then I have the song "Defying Gravity" like an earworm all the way back upstairs and into my room.

I'm even humming as I get out of my dirty sweats and *Oxford Comma Preservation Society* T-shirt and into my nicest nightgown, a barely worn Christmas present from one of those people you hardly know who send gifts every year. Aunt Somebody from Somewhere. I want to look nice when Mom finds me, so I brush my hair, too. Then I sit on the edge of the bed and take a bunch of ibuprofens with some orange juice. It takes three times before I've taken it all. I wait a few minutes for something to happen. But nothing does, so I arrange myself neatly on my bed, even making sure my hair fans out dramatically on my pillow.

I feel almost excited because any minute now, it will be over. All the pain and sadness, yes, but mostly all the numbness that has taken me over. Waiting for this overdose to start is the most excited I've felt in a long time. Which is pathetic. I finally start to feel nauseous, and my ears are ringing and maybe I'm a little dizzy. *Here it comes, here it comes, here it comes . . .*

I have to stop thinking about these stupid things I did. *Stop!* I scream in my brain.

Maggie has her head tilted, studying me, and the small room smells like pizza, and I almost can't breathe.

"Thanks," I say. And then, "For the pizza and everything."

When I'm almost out the door, Maggie comes right up behind me. "Why don't you switch to garden duty?"

"Oh, I really like laundry duty," I say.

She levels those eyes straight at me. "You wanted pizza," she says. "And I got you pizza."

"But sure. Garden is good, too," I say.

CHAPTER FIFTEEN

IN WHICH I BECOME ATOMIC NUMBER 76

I show up for garden duty wearing the required ugly dark green Crocs and holding one of the big wicker baskets. In October, the vegetables are pretty limited: broccoli, brussels sprouts, beets. And of course, enormous pumpkins have shown up, looking bright and happy and orange. Standing out there looking at the pumpkin patch makes me sad, deeply sad. I'm remembering us going with Virginia's family to pick pumpkins and walk through a corn maze and drink apple cider. When we got home, we carved jack-o'-lanterns and ate her mom's famous chili and cornbread. We didn't do this just a few times; we did it every year until Halley died. Then Virginia moved away and got a different family and

Mom and I didn't even mention pumpkins.

But here they are, dozens of them. I get this terrible urge to destroy every one of them. I drop the wicker basket and stomp through the rows between the broccoli and beets to the pumpkin patch. Up close they aren't as beautiful. Some of them have green warts growing on them and some are misshapen, and some are skinny instead of plump and round. I start to kick them, knocking them one at a time off their vine. At first they just kind of topple over, but then I'm kicking them harder and they go sailing through the air. I probably destroyed ten or twelve before I hear someone yelling for me to stop.

A girl is running toward me. I think it must be Maggie, because she's the reason I'm out here instead of in my warm laundry room. But as she gets closer, I see that this girl has short dark hair and glasses. Most definitely not Maggie. It's Liliana, a quiet girl who hardly ever says anything, but she is yelling now, loud.

"They can't live off the vine," she says when she reaches me, panting.

She has a soft voice, when she isn't yelling.

"I know," I tell her. "I want them to die."

I rev up to kick another pumpkin, but she grabs my arm, which knocks me off-balance slightly.

"Once," she says quietly, "I removed the legs of a spider."

"Why?"

She shrugs. "To be cruel."

I look away from her and back at all the pumpkins. I was never much of a carver, so my jack-o'-lanterns were always basic: triangle eyes and nose, jagged grin. But Halley turned pumpkins into beautiful things. The last time we all went to the pumpkin patch, instead of carving her pumpkin she carefully shaved off the skin, revealing a witch on a broomstick. When it was lit it was so lovely that Celeste asked Halley to do hers, too. She made a bat on that one. "Want me to do yours?" she asked me. I was hacking away clumsily at my pumpkin, but I said no, anyway. She looked so hopeful when she asked me, but I wanted to be mean to her, and I was.

"Where's Maggie?" I ask without turning around. "I'm supposed to be out here with Maggie."

"Didn't you hear?"

That makes me turn around.

"She got sent away," Liliana says.

"Home?"

She shakes her head. "To one of those wilderness schools? In Montana or somewhere like that?" Liliana says.

Then she speaks even more softly. "They found gin or something in her room," she says. "There are cameras, like in the halls, and I guess they saw her or something."

Did they see me sneaking into Maggie's room? Are they going to send me to a wilderness school in Montana? I don't know what's going to happen next, and I don't like not knowing that. In that instant, all I want is to go home. To be in my own bed or even watching *Masterpiece Theatre* with Mom.

I just drop to the ground, too broken to even cry. My body seems to have turned to lead, or something heavier than lead. Osmium. Isn't that what Mr. Buck, the chemistry teacher, said was the heaviest material in the world? I am osmium, too heavy to get up or move at all. So heavy that I am sinking into the dirt. I can feel it breaking apart beneath me from my weight. My head drops because I can't hold it up. Mr. Buck said osmium is rarely used because it's so toxic and volatile. Like me.

I don't know how long I sit there before two shadows fall over me. I can't lift my head but with great effort I can raise my eyes. Liliana is there looking terrified and beside her is Mrs. Van Der Berg, the person who runs the group sessions. Mrs. Van Der Berg doesn't seem frightened, she seems confused. She's an MSW, which means she has a master's in social work, and she acts so proud of that. Also, she's from the Netherlands and has a habit of saying "Ja, ja," after someone finishes, which is either totally charming or totally annoying depending on my mood.

But what she is saying now is, "Are you hurt? Can you stand?"

I want to tell her I can't. I want to tell her about osmium and toxicity and volatility. I want to tell her that I actually wanted a cat on my pumpkin that October night, but I was too jealous.

"We're going to help you get up," Mrs. Van Der Berg says.

It takes all my energy, but I manage to nod.

"Okay, good. Liliana," Mrs. Van Der berg says, "take her other arm."

That's when I realize she's gripping me under my right armpit, and then Liliana has her hands around my left upper arm, and the two of them are trying to lift me off the ground but they can't because I am osmium. Basically, my feet drag through the pumpkin patch and then through the row between the broccoli and the beans and across the grass and dirt to the door that leads into the basement. At one point I lose one of the ugly dark green Crocs.

"The nurse is waiting for you," Mrs. Van Der Berg says. "She's going to take care of you."

Osmium is the heaviest metal on earth, I try to say. But she is just opening the door and dragging me across the threshold, Liliana still holding on tight.

Why don't they understand? Why doesn't anyone?

CHAPTER SIXTEEN

IN WHICH I AM A WEEPING WILLOW

Nothing can get me out of bed. Somehow, I was put in my pajamas and into bed and now they can't move me. They tried cajoling and commiserating and threatening. They had Maeve try to talk to me, and then Ms. Myrtle, who they apparently believe I have some kind of relationship with. I do not. But I refuse to budge.

To be accurate, I am not asleep. I just have my eyes closed and my heart and brain shut off. I am not thinking or feeling or doing anything. Instead of osmium, I am now a tree. Outside this room there is a gloriously sad weeping willow tree, bending its branches to the ground like rivers of tears. I am that tree. I am sad and bending downward.

I feel things: the change of temperature when the old radiators come on one especially cold night, the buzzing electricity of tension in the room, the subtle differences in lights turned on and off, footsteps moving past or pausing or entering. I smell things: Maeve's cheap coconut shampoo when she returns from the shower, Ms. Myrtle's heavily floral perfume, the vague odors of meals, of bacon and tomato soup and spaghetti sauce. But I don't open my eyes or pull my covers over me. I just lie there.

Then one day—three, four, five days later?—there are footsteps (sneakers; I've learned to tell the difference) and the door opening slowly and the squeak and drop of the bed as someone sits. The smell that mingles with the room's stale air is familiar. Patchouli. And the hand that tenderly touches my cheek is, too.

Mom.

My eyelids flutter but stay closed.

"I've come to take you home, sweetie," Mom says, her palm still on my cheek. "I guess this was a bad idea."

I wait for relief or even elation to wash over me. But nothing.

"So I'm going to pack your things and someone is

bringing you a light lunch because apparently you haven't eaten in days. And then you're going to sit up and eat that light lunch and you don't even have to change your clothes. You're just going to walk out of here with me and get in the car and come home."

The bed rises slightly when she gets up and I hear drawers open and close, the closet door open, clothes being swept off coat hangers. A new smell. Chicken soup?

"All right now, Clementine," Mom says. "Soup and saltines."

"I told you," I hear Mrs. Van Der Berg say, "she will not move."

Mom's sneakered footsteps come closer and then she is tugging me up and settling me against the headboard, the way she used to line up my dolls on the shelf. My head droops and she pulls it back up from the top, which makes me think of my doll that had a hole in her head and inside that hole was extra hair so you could tug it out and give her longer hair, braid it, or make a ponytail, then shove it back in so her hair was a pixie cut again.

"There you go," Mom says, slightly out of breath from all the tugging.

Mrs. Van Der Berg pries my lips open with the tip of a warm metal spoon. Some broth goes in but most of it dribbles down my chin. It doesn't matter. She keeps sticking that spoon against my teeth and in no time I am warm and wet and smell like chicken soup. Most of it is on my face and T-shirt.

"They're sending a wheelchair," she says.

An awkward silence descends, a silence I can feel, a heavy damp blanket of it.

"As you know," Mrs. Van Der Berg says after a little bit, "Sandy Point has a very high success rate with girls like Clementine. She just refuses to participate."

"Yes," Mom says sternly. "I know."

What she sees is that I have toppled over, more or less. My head and the top of my torso are bent so that my hair is in my lap and my eyes, if I were to open them, would be looking at my belly button. I spread and droop my arms like weeping willow branches.

"Our opinion is that her behavior is performative," Mrs. Van Der Berg says. Then she adds, in case Mom can't understand multisyllabic words, "For attention."

"Yes," Mom says again.

Finally, the clatter of the wheelchair approaches and I hear its wheels stop by the bed and a new set of arms lifts me and plunks me down onto it.

There's the pull of what feels like a seat belt and then the click of the buckle and then I'm off, zipping down the hall, across the wooden lobby floor, and out the front door into a cold bright morning.

I shiver. I stink of soup. My hair is matted. I have BO. But I am going home.

⸻⸙⸻

"I thought it would help," Mom says in the car. Then she adds, "I hoped it would help."

"Sorry," I mumble.

"Kicking pumpkins? Hugging the clothes dryer?" Mom asks in a way that I know doesn't require an answer.

"Remember," I croak, my voice rusty from lack of use, "that story about this woman who loved weeping willow trees and her husband planted one for her as a surprise?"

"Um, no," Mom says, confused.

"And then she got sick with something, maybe leukemia, and she died really quick, and she never got to see that tree. The title of the story was 'My Willow Weeps for Me,' because those trees look like they're crying."

"What does this have to do with anything, sweetie? I'm not following."

Why does this make so much sense to me and none whatsoever to her?

The car stops and I see that we are home and a warm, wonderful feeling spreads through me.

I grab Mom's arm and she turns to look at me.

"You told me that when I was a baby and I wouldn't sleep you used to put me in my car seat on top of the dryer and turn the dryer on," I say.

"That was your father," she says. "He used to do that."

The streetlights are on even though it's only five o'clock because it's November. We sit in the almost dark, without getting out of the car.

"Is that why you were hugging the dryer?" Mom says.

"I don't know. It just felt good. Safe."

Mom tries to hug me but it's awkward to hug in the car. "Come on, let's get inside," she says.

I'm surprised there's a bunch of that fake harvest corn hanging on the front door, and that inside on the table where we put our keys in a little ceramic bowl Halley made in summer camp there's a straw cornucopia with fake autumn vegetables artfully arranged in it. While I was away hiking and journaling and doing other people's laundry, Mom was decorating the house for Thanksgiving.

Mom appears in front of me. "I'll make us some dinner while you unpack, okay?"

I turn back around and head out the door. But halfway to the car, I realize my shaky legs and heavy self will not, cannot make it there. So I drop to the cool, damp grass and stretch out on it. I'm cold because I don't have on a coat or even shoes, but I don't care. I just curl up tight.

The light shifts to evening autumn light, which is kind of silvery. The clouds look lower in the sky. A cat saunters over to me and steps right onto my chest, like I'm a log or something. It's a big fat calico with yellow eyes that are boring into me. The cat headbutts my chin. Then it settles down right on me, purring like a motor that needs oil.

At some point, though, the cat gets up and I feel the weight of it lift, and the warmth from it vanish. I slowly pull myself up to standing. It is officially evening, moving toward night. I make my shaky way to the car and get my duffel bags of stuff and lug them up and into the house, where I drop them right inside the door and follow the smells of something cooking into the kitchen.

Mom is standing at the stove stirring something with a long-handled wooden spoon. The pasta pot is boiling beside it noisily.

"It's just jarred sauce," she says apologetically, "but I added some Italian seasonings."

"Smells good," I say, suddenly famished.

"Five more minutes," Mom says, testing a strand of spaghetti. "Time for you to set the table."

I take two plates out of the cupboard and put them on the new orange woven placemats. The basket that holds the napkins has orange napkins in it that I also don't recognize. I fold them and put them to the left of the plate with a fork on top. There's a weird pottery vase in the middle of the table with cattails in it along with what looks like wheat.

"You've been decorating the house?" I say.

Mom faces me, holding the pasta bowl with the steaming sauce-covered spaghetti in it.

"I wanted it to look happy," she says.

I wait for her to explain more, but she just puts the bowl on the table and pulls a salad out of the fridge with a bottle of Italian dressing.

"Dig in," Mom says when she sits down.

I fill my dish with spaghetti and even salad, which is iceberg lettuce with tomato wedges and pinwheels of cucumbers and shredded carrot, just the way I like it. Mom has been known to make a salad with too-spicy arugula or even quinoa, but tonight she made just the kind I like. Lots of people don't like when sauce bleeds onto other food on their plate, but I actually like that, so the edges of my salad turn oily from dressing and red from sauce and I save them for last.

I eat three helpings, even though Mom eats only half of what she put on her plate. No salad, just the cucumbers.

"That kid called. Miles?" she says. "Also, Jayden?"

"They did?"

Mom nods. "And that sweet kid from City of Angels wrote to you. I put the letter on your nightstand."

Jude. I forgot I wrote to him during the letter-writing activity.

"I didn't know you had so many boyfriends," she says.

"Well, Jude is, like, twelve. And Miles is just my *friend*. And Jayden is . . ." I almost say *Jayden is trouble*, but instead I say, ". . . a scholar athlete."

"That's a good thing? Or not?"

"Not," I say.

"After you load the dishwasher," Mom says, "you want to watch *Top Chef*?"

"There's a new one?"

"Houston," she says.

"Okay."

So that's what I do. I load the dishwasher and take a shower and then I plop on my beanbag and watch as all these chefs do ridiculous things for the title of Top Chef. Mom and I each pick our favorite, even though I don't actually have one.

When the show ends, after we watch the previews for next week, I say, "I'm glad I'm home. And, Mom, I promise I'll try to do better. To be better."

"I know you will," she says. "And, sweetie?"

"Anything."

"School tomorrow."

I think about those hikes and those groups sessions and Maggie and her gin off at a wilderness school and the idea of school, even my school, actually sounds pretty good.

CHAPTER SEVENTEEN

IN WHICH I HAVE APPENDICITIS

I can't explain what happened, just that something did. Maybe all those group therapy sessions and book discussion groups and long hikes did help? I went to bed and slept the night through and when my alarm woke me up playing "Good Morning Starshine" from *Hair*, I only hit SNOOZE twice. Thirty minutes later, I'm popping two frozen waffles into the toaster while Mom gets ready to leave for work. She comes in the kitchen, dangling her keys, watching me dip my waffles into strawberry jam and then fake maple syrup.

"Okay," she says, nodding like she's figured something out. "I'll be home at three."

Mother's hours, I remember. Nine to three.

"Maybe we can have a nice girls' chat, what do you say?" Mom says.

"A girls' chat?"

"You can tell me more about this boy . . . Jayden?"

"There's nothing to tell," I say, thinking this is kind of coming out of nowhere.

"And I'll tell you about things," Mom says.

"Things?"

She shrugs. "Oh, never mind."

"Okay. Have a good day," I say, and offer a smile that feels almost normal instead of like a wild animal baring her teeth.

"You too, kiddo," she says, and she squeezes my shoulder as she walks past me.

After she leaves, I shower and wash my hair and put on clean clothes that I haven't seen in almost three weeks. I jam my books and stuff into my backpack and leave for school. What I don't do, and maybe this is the key to my productivity, is think about Halley. I just keep moving, one foot in front of the other. *Be in the moment,* someone at Sandy Point said. At the time, I rolled my eyes because the place was such a weird combination of New Age and military school. But now *Be in the moment* seems exactly right. Wake up. Eat breakfast. Get ready. *Go!*

While I was away, the beginnings of a New England winter started. The air is chillier and the trees are all bare except for a few straggling leaves clinging on for dear life. Like me, I think. Then I immediately reprimand myself. *You are not a leaf, Clementine. You are a girl on her way to school.*

A car slows and for a moment I think it must be a kidnapper, ready to snatch me and do who knows what. I walk faster, head down.

"Hey! Clem!" a guy calls.

No one, but no one, ever calls me Clem. I whip my head around to say something salty but when I do I see that it's Jayden, Scholar Athlete, leaning across the front seat of a silvery-green Prius, his head stuck out the passenger window.

The door pops open. "Hop in," he said.

I can't remember how I last felt about him, so I get in the car.

"Where've you been? You missed the whole *Crucible* thing," he says.

"I was in the hospital," I say.

"Whoa. Like appendicitis?"

I have no idea why he thinks this, but I jump on it. "Yes," I say. "Appendicitis!" I throw in a slight wince, because if I had my appendix out ten days ago, my stomach must hurt, right? Then I add, "It really hurt."

Jayden nods. "But now you have a cute little scar," he says.

"Well," I say, "yes."

"Cool, cool, cool," he says.

I decide that when anyone asks where I've been, I will stick with the appendicitis story. Probably no one even noticed I was gone, but just in case.

"Hey," Jayden says, and he taps my arm lightly, "how about skipping?"

"Skipping?"

He laughs. "School," he says. "Skipping school."

"Scholar athletes do things like that?"

"Not usually," he admits.

"Maybe another time. It's my first day back and I've got to catch up."

For some reason, the memory of the day I skipped

school and met Jude at the cemetery crowds its way into my brain. We talked about our dead sisters, and grief, and all sorts of serious things. But I have decided not to think about Halley today, so I imagine pushing a giant boulder in front of my brain, blocking out the memory of that day.

"I could give you a ride home after school," Jayden is saying. "Except I have practice so it wouldn't be until five. But maybe you can come and watch?"

"Wait a minute," I say. "The last time I saw you, you acted like you didn't even know me. In the lunchroom."

"I don't remember that."

"Well, I do." I consider getting out of the car, but the school is right up ahead, so I sit looking out the window until we are in the student parking lot.

Jayden pulls into a spot, but he doesn't turn off the car right away.

"Okay," he says, tapping the steering wheel with his long fingers, "of course I remember. It's just that around my friends—"

"You're a jerk?"

"No! Well, maybe. Not a jerk, exactly, but, I don't know, the way they expect me to be."

"Which means not friends with someone who isn't cool," I say.

"I guess," he admits. "I'm sorry I acted that way. I don't like myself when I act like such a stereotype of 'popular kid.'"

"Fair," I say.

"Okay," Jayden says.

"Okay," I say.

⤙⚡⤚

"Appendicitis," I tell Miles.

"Appendicitis," I tell Samantha, whose eyes widen. "You had, like, *surgery*?" she said.

"Appendicitis," I tell Agnes when she comes up to me in the lunch line.

"Really," she says, my first doubter.

"I have a scar," I say.

"Did they remove it laparoscopically?" Agnes asks, narrowing her eyes at me. "That's what they did when my brother had appendicitis."

"Of course." I try to sound haughty, even though I'm pumping ketchup onto my hot dog.

"So where's your scar?"

I roll my eyes. "Where my appendix was. Obviously."

Agnes looks satisfied. "Laparoscopic surgery goes through your *belly button.*"

"Why would I lie about having my appendix out? I mean, seriously."

I grab a wiggling bowl of red Jell-O from the dessert table, take a deep breath, and prepare for the walk of shame across the cafeteria. Agnes sticks close to me.

"Because maybe you were in the psych ward again?" she's saying. As she walks, she's doing little jumps up and down on her toes, like she's excited.

I stop walking and stare at her hard. "I was not," I say. Which is the truth.

"Maybe you—"

To my utter disbelief, Jayden is waving me over to the scholar athlete table.

"I had my appendix out," I say. "Laparoscopically," I add, hoping I pronounced it right. Then I turn my back on Agnes and walk toward something normal and good, even if stereotypical.

On my way, I pass Miles, who is sitting as usual with

the math nerds, working out Algebra 2 problems with a group of other math geniuses. When I told them about having my appendix out, I felt a little guilty for lying to them, especially when they said, "Ouch! Are you okay?" So I give a thumbs-up as I walk by and keep living in the moment all the way to the scholar athlete table. Jayden pats the seat next to him.

"Hey, dudes, you all know Clementine, right?" he says. "She just had her appendix out."

Everybody murmurs some kind of acknowledgment, but otherwise they just keep on talking about whatever they were talking about before I got there. College essays. Early decision versus early action. APush, which is AP US History, the most dreaded class in the entire school. The football team. The basketball team. The ice hockey team. Proving that they are indeed *scholar athletes*. I eat my hot dog and my Jell-O, and when the bell rings and they all stand up, I do, too. That's when Jayden finally looks at me.

"You going to watch practice?"

"No."

"Please?"

"No."

"Pretty please?"

I laugh and shake my head.

"With a cherry on top?"

"Stop," I say.

"So that's a yes?"

"That's a maybe," I say, surprising myself.

Just like that, he's gone and I'm standing alone at the cafeteria entrance. And in another just like that, Miles appears.

"We started a poetry unit."

"Finally, something I like," I say.

"I can help you catch up. You missed kind of a lot."

"That would be great, Miles. Thanks."

"Can you come to my house tonight? It's just Emily Dickinson and Robert Frost."

Ugh. Robert Frost. I'll never think of him the same way after our visit to Vermont last month.

"Sure," I say.

I watch Miles walk away, toward a few kids waiting for them by the vending machine. I only recognize one of them, Astra, president of the LGBTQ+ club. For the first time, I see Miles differently. Maybe they're more like me than I thought, someone trying to figure out who they are. Funny, now that I think of it, Jayden is kind of that way, too, a little uncomfortable in his scholar athlete role. For the first time, I wonder if everybody here is trying to figure out who they are, if maybe I'm not the only one.

My epiphany is interrupted by a red-faced teacher with a whistle around her neck and a line of girls all wearing some kind of sports uniform and carrying sticks.

"Where are you supposed to be, missy?"

"Um. English."

"Hmmph," she says. "This doesn't look like an English classroom. It looks like a cafeteria!" Her face gets redder still. "Do you have a hall pass?"

I shake my head. "I'm just on my way," I say.

She waits. The line of kids shifts around, bored.

"I just had my appendix out so I'm moving kind of slow." My hand drifts to the right side of my stomach. I hope appendixes are on the right.

"Then you should have an elevator pass!"

"Okay."

"Go to the office and get an elevator pass."

"Okay," I say again, and hurry away.

I didn't realize appendicitis had so many benefits. In no time, I have an elevator pass and the elevator is whooshing me up to the second floor and my English class.

I consider using my fake appendicitis again as an excuse for being late to Ms. Quigley, but the teachers probably know the truth. I whisper, "Sorry," and wave my elevator pass.

Ms. Quigley says, "Welcome back, Clementine. Glad you're feeling better."

I place my left hand on the right side of my stomach because the whole class is watching me as I walk to my seat.

"So," Ms. Quigley says, "whose woods *are* these?"

I can do this.

CHAPTER EIGHTEEN

IN WHICH HOPE IS THE THING WITH FEATHERS

Football practice is so boring that I can't stay for more than fifteen minutes. Plus, Lacy and Casey are both there giving me the stink eye and whispering to their friend group: Olivia, Lily, Alice, and Cee-Cee. So all those other girls are also giving me the stink eye. Three of them—I'm not really sure who is who—have on their cheerleader uniforms and periodically, when something happens on the field, they jump to their feet and shake their pom-poms. At one point, Jayden looks over at the stands and waves to me. Or I think he waves to me except then one of the cheerleaders waves back to him.

I zip up my coat and start to collect my stuff.

"Leaving so soon?" Lacy or Casey asks me.

"It just started, you know," the other one says.

"How's your appendix, anyway?" one of the cheerleaders asks, narrowing her eyes.

"Better," I say. "Once they take them out, you're pretty much fine."

A non-cheerleader says, "Funny that after you get expelled from school for beating up Lacy—"

I say, "I didn't beat her up. And I didn't get expelled. I got detention."

"Oh, right," she says. "And wrote the lamest apology letter in the history of apology letters."

"Whatever," I say with a shrug.

"What are you doing here, anyway?" Lacy asks me.

"Leaving," I mutter.

"Since when are you interested in sports?" she continues.

"I'm not. Jayden asked me to come," I say. Then I add, "He's a scholar athlete."

"Well, he likes *me*," one of the cheerleaders says. "So I doubt he asked *you* anywhere."

I have started down the bleachers, but I stop when she says that. "Well, he did. And he kissed me, too," I say, puckering my lips. "Right here. So maybe he doesn't like you."

"Oh please!" Lacy says.

But the cheerleader is considering what I said. "When was this?"

"Ask him," I say, and continue down the bleachers.

"Liar!" one of them yells after me.

"Is this one of your hallucinations?" another one shouts.

"Take care of your appendix!" someone else calls, and they all laugh.

I want to run home and get in bed because I am living in the moment and this one's awful. I am not having a nice day after all.

According to Miles, we have to choose either Robert Frost or Emily Dickinson and write a five-page paper on their life and an analysis of one poem, and then we have to give an oral presentation.

We are sitting in their McMansion, eating Cheez-Its and microwave popcorn and drinking grapefruit-flavored

LaCroix. The can says PAMPLEMOUSSE, which makes us both laugh and forces us to use that word incorrectly whenever we have the opportunity.

"I'm going to do Emily Pamplemousse," I say, "because I have an aversion to Robert Frost." I think of that visit to Virginia again and her dumb stepfather quoting Frost and making us walk to his cabin.

"Me too," Miles says.

Off the kitchen is an entire room of snacks and there's an extra refrigerator filled with all kinds of drinks. When I opened my LaCroix in there, Miles took my arm and said, "No, no, we don't eat or drink in here." And then led me to the proper kitchen where we sit now at a counter made out of sea glass.

"'She developed a penchant for white clothes,'" I read from Wikipedia. "What do you think that was about?"

Miles shrugs. "I don't know. She was just such a . . . pamplemousse."

The more I read about Emily Dickinson, the more I love her. A recluse. Hated guests. Troubled by "the deepening menace of death." What I realize is that if I lived in Amherst, Massachusetts, between 1830 and 1886, surely Emily Dickinson would have been my best friend. We would have spent hours hiding from people in our white dresses, pondering death.

"I think I'll analyze 'I'm Nobody! Who are you?'" Miles says after we've both sat reading her poems for a while.

I've read about ten poems so far and I'm not that wild about them. So many dashes and they're so short. Maybe I should have picked Robert Frost.

"We have to consider rhyme, meter, and theme in the analysis," Miles says.

Then I read a poem that I really like: "Because I could not stop for Death." This one has it all—personification, six stanzas with four lines each (a quatrain), symbolism, irony. It's perfect. Except for the fact that it's about death, and if I stand up in front of the class and read a poem about death, I'll get mocked for the rest of the year. Still, the more I read it, the more I see in it.

"Oh, that's a good one," Miles says, looking at what I'm reading.

"But kind of dark?"

"I don't know. She *doesn't* stop for death."

"But he kindly stops for her," I say, pointing to the second line.

Miles shrugs. "It's about immortality, though?"

I shake my head. There's no way I can do this poem out loud in front of Lacy and Casey.

"I need something more hopeful," I say, flipping the pages.

Even as I say it, I wonder why I care what these kids think about me. They already think I'm a weirdo, or worse. I'm a person who slapped a girl and disappeared from school for almost three weeks. Plus, there's the dead sister, and the overdosing on Advil.

"'Hope is the thing with feathers,'" Miles is saying.

"What does that mean?" I ask, suddenly feeling terrible, like I'm the Wicked Witch of the West melting and melting.

Miles slides their book over to me. "A poem. About hope."

I read the poem, and it doesn't have any of the power or symbolism of the death one. It's almost singsongy. Even as I read it silently, I can see the rhyme scheme clear as anything:

a b c b, a b a b, a b b b.

"I heard somewhere that any Emily Dickinson poem can be sung to the tune of 'The Yellow Rose of Texas,'" Miles says.

I look down at the hope poem.

"'Hope is the thing with feathers,'" I sing to the tune of "The Yellow Rose of Texas," "'that perches in the soul'!"

Miles joins in on the next two lines and then we are laughing too hard to sing anymore. But when we catch our breath, we both let out a loud long "Pamplemoooooose!", howling like a pair of wolves.

A few days later I am standing in front of my English class reciting "Hope is the thing with feathers," and saying, "Emily Dickinson wrote this poem in 1861. It is a lyric poem with a rhyme scheme of a b c b, a b a b, a b b b. It has her usual long dashes for breaks. Dickinson uses extended metaphor. She sets up the metaphor in the first two lines: 'Hope is the thing with feathers - / That perches in the soul -.' Then she tells us that the bird sings, remains unabashed in the storm, and can be found everywhere, meaning that even through all kinds of hardships there is still hope. And that hope lives in our souls, during storms and rain and cold."

The class is dead quiet when I finish. I see Lacy and Casey glance at each other, and I see Miles grinning at me, and Samantha has tears in her eyes, and Ms. Quigley's head is bobbing up and down and she says, "Well, brava, Clementine Marsh. Brava."

I look at Ms. Quigley in her orange sweatshirt that has THANKFUL written in yellow all over it and Miles with bangs in their eyes and Samantha smiling up at me with her hot-pink braces and something deep in me stirs but I can't tell what it is. I want to think it's that bird perched in my soul starting to maybe sing.

CHAPTER NINETEEN

IN WHICH I COUNT
THE MOMENTS

It gets harder to stay in the moment when my mind and heart and even my soul (if there's such a thing) keep getting challenged. I'll have a moment like I did in English class, but then I'll have a night full of creepy sounds and bad thoughts. I'll FaceTime Samantha to help her with her poetry presentation, and she'll make me laugh by continually calling Robert Frost Robert Frosty. Then I can't sleep because all I can think about is how much Halley loved that *Frosty the Snowman* cartoon and we used to watch it all year, not just in winter.

A couple of days after my poetry presentation, I had another roller-coaster day: Samantha was waiting for me at lunch, and I walked into the cafeteria with her, and we got our food together and carried our trays over to a table. It felt so good to be with someone nice, who makes me laugh, and who seems to really like me. But then when I got home I almost had a panic attack because in the mail was a letter for Halley.

When I saw her name on the pink envelope, my hands started to shake. I didn't recognize the return address— Sabrina Martinez in San Juan, Puerto Rico. I considered just throwing it away, but then I thought about Sabrina Martinez in San Juan, Puerto Rico, waiting forever for a reply that would never come. I tore the letter open and there, on pink paper in loopy handwriting, read:

Dear Halley,

I found you on the dearpenpal website and saw that you want a pen pal who lives somewhere beautiful and tropical. I live in Puerto Rico and it's exactly what you describe you want. There are palm trees and beautiful beaches and rainforests and lots more! I am also eleven years old, just like you (math whiz! I see that you were nine when *you signed up a couple years ago!), and I also like art and reading and that Frosty the Snowman movie! I hope we can be pen pals? Please say yes!*

Your Pen Pal (I hope),
Sabrina

I didn't know that Halley had signed up for a pen pal on some website, but it didn't surprise me. She always did things like that. She adopted a manatee through a savethemanatee website, got nail polish from trytheseonyournails, and signed up for Pottery Barn Kids online newsletters just so she could plan fake bedrooms and TV rooms. Now some kid in San Juan, Puerto Rico, was hoping to be Halley's pen pal.

By the time Mom comes home from work with her usual bags of craft stuff from Forget-Me-Knot, I'm lying on my bed with all the lights off trying not to go to a dark place.

Mom bustles in, already talking about the Swedish embroidery kit she got with her discount.

"I think we'll go out for dinner tonight, sweetie," she

says, switching on the bedside lamp. "There are some things I want to talk about. Exciting things."

There's a pause and then she says, "Oh no. What happened?"

I wonder if I should show her the letter, which I have clutched in my hand, or if that will make her sad. It seems like Mom and I are always circling each other, trying to keep sadness at bay.

She sits on the bed and without thinking about it another second, I hand her the letter.

Mom looks confused at first, too, but then she reads it and I see her heart breaking a little.

"Isn't that just like Halley to sign up for a pen pal somewhere tropical?" she says, smiling a sad little smile.

"Should we tell her?"

Mom folds the letter back up and tucks it in the envelope. "I don't think so," she says. "That's a lot for an eleven-year-old who just wants a pen pal."

It's a lot for a fourteen-year-old, too, I think, but I don't say anything.

"How about pizza?" Mom says. "You don't seem like you're up for going out tonight."

"Okay," I say.

"We can talk another time soon."

"Okay," I say.

I don't wonder what exciting things she wants to talk about until after she's gone. Or maybe it's just her Swedish embroidery kit. Mom gets way too excited about crafts projects these days.

⸙

One of the tips Mrs. Van Der Berg gave us was to write down all of our thoughts, good ones and bad ones. I dig out a notebook I got for Christmas when I was nine or ten, meaning it's sparkly and pink and has a unicorn with a rainbow-colored horn dancing across the cover, and I take it to school the next day so I can start to write down moments. At first, I don't number them but then I decide that it's easier to keep track of them if I number them and also to remind myself of how hard it is to actually do this. *Stay in the moment.*

When I walk past Lacy and Casey's lockers, I hear them whispering. "She's trying to act all normal now."

Gloria from City of Angels would say: "That's

ridiculous. What is normal, anyway? There's no such thing."

I want to stop and tell them this. I want to ask them if they think they're normal? Seriously?

But instead, I write: Walking past Lacy and Casey's lockers, I hear them whispering. "She's trying to act all normal now."

One of them calls after me. "What are you, a reporter or something?"

"Are you literally taking notes about us?" the other one says, indignant.

Instead of answering, I write: One of them calls after me. "What are you, a reporter or something?"

"Are you literally taking notes about us?" the other one says, indignant.

By last period, I have fifty-one moments written down. None of them are good ones.

11. During lunch, Agnes asks me to name the Disney princesses. Again. I try to ignore her, but she starts to badger me. "You STILL don't know them?"

27. I see Jayden and smile at him, and he looks at me like he has never seen me before. Like I'm a stranger smiling in his direction. "Hello?" I say. He keeps walking. (Note to self: I think technically these are two moments.)

42. I am minding my own business, sitting in history class and trying to think about the in-class writing assignment on Archduke Ferdinand when Mr. Beasley says, out of nowhere, "Remember, people, the past is never dead. It's not even past." Mr. Beasley, he of the bow ties and patterned suspenders and funny socks (Pizza slices! Smiley faces! Cats!), is no doubt saying this as a clue to what he wants us to write about, but Samantha speaks for all of us when she asks him what that means. "If the past isn't past," she says, her eyes like spinning Frisbees, "then are we, like, time traveling?" Mr. Beasley sighs, long and exaggerated. "Think about it, people." That's what he

calls us. People. Samantha looks even more terrified, but I am living in the moment, so I do what he suggests. I think about it.

43. "The past is never dead. It's not even past." It must mean we have to confront our history. We can't ignore it.

44. A tsunami surges in my chest, wild and uncontrollable, and at the center of it is Halley, dead.

45. I make a sound, like I'm strangling, because I am strangling. On the past that's not even past.

46. Tittering. Everywhere. Whispers.

47. "Clementine Marsh," Mr. Beasley says, "you may be excused." Did I ask to be excused? I did not. He is telling me to leave.

48. I leave history class.

49. I sit down right in the hall and start to cry.
   What is more than crying? Sobbing. I sob.
   Then more than sobbing. Wailing. I wail.

50. A teacher I don't know comes out and says,
   "Keep it down." I guess she thought I was just
   making a racket because when she realizes
   I'm wailing, she scurries over to me and asks
   what she can do. She has on white sneakers
   that look like jumbo marshmallows and
   nude-colored pantyhose. I know this because I
   don't look up at her, just at her feet, which
   are eye level. Her question makes me wail
   harder. (Note to self: Look up word for
   something more than wailing.) What can she
   do? What can she do? What can anyone do?

51. I look it up. Worse than wailing is keening:
   the action of wailing in grief for a dead
   person.

CHAPTER TWENTY

IN WHICH WE ARE
ALMOST WAY BACK HERE

"Sweetie, you're going to be late," Mom says the next morning.

She's standing in the doorway of my bedroom. I can tell from the direction her voice is coming from.

Ever since I read that dumb letter the other day, I've been off course. Despite what Mrs. Van Der Berg said, writing things down didn't help. It made everything feel worse. Last night, Mom made chicken stir-fry with snow peas and peanuts, one of my all-time favorite things. She doesn't make it much because it takes so long to cut everything up in bite-size pieces.

But last night she said, "We have to celebrate how well you're doing!" and I felt so guilty because I feel myself slip sliding away from well that I ate seconds and talked about Samantha like we were best friends just to make Mom feel happy.

But when she said, "Let's knit together or something and talk!" I told her I had too much homework and went to my room and right into bed.

"Oh, Clementine," Mom says, "we're not going back here, are we? Remember how well you're doing? Remember your new friend Samantha and how we talked about having her come sleep over?"

I can feel her waiting. It feels like electricity buzzing.

I take the pillow off my face. "I'm getting up," I say, though my body—leaden, inert, frozen in place—doesn't agree. "I'm good."

"Good!" she says, relieved.

"I'm getting up," I say again. "And I'm going to school."

"O-*kay*!" Mom says in a way that makes me think of that song in *Oklahoma* that Halley and I used to sing, pretending to ride horses around the living room. *And when we say, Yeeow! Ayipioeeay! We're only sayin', you're doin' fine, Oklahoma! Oklahoma, OK!* Mom and Virginia's mom took us to see that musical at the Performing Arts

Center and we all thought it was terrible, except for our moms. They loved it. *It's Rodgers and Hammerstein, girls! How can you not love it?*

"She smiles," Mom says, still in the doorway.

"I was thinking about *Oklahoma*."

"Remember how much you girls loved it?" she says. "'Chicks and ducks and geese better scurry, When I take you out in the surrey!'" Mom sings in a bad Oklahoma twang. "That was your favorite."

"I didn't have a favorite," I say, willing my legs to swing out of bed.

"Me, I always liked 'Oh, What a Beautiful Mornin'.' That's a good one."

Legs cooperate but drop to the floor with a thud.

"Frozen waffles okay? Again?" Mom says, but she doesn't wait for an answer. Just like that, she's gone, presumably to put some waffles in the toaster.

I change my shirt but not my sweatpants. I keep on the same socks, too. I ponder if we are all the way back here again. Back here means: Sleeping all the time. Not eating much. Skipping school. Breaking rules. But no. I am upright, in a clean shirt. I brush my hair. I used to do it a hundred times because I read in a magazine it makes hair shinier. Now I basically untangle the top part and don't really deal with the underneath snarls. Where does that put us on the *back here* continuum?

As I pour fake maple syrup onto my under-toasted waffles, Mom whizzes past.

"I'll drop you off at school," she says over her shoulder. "On my way to work," she adds, as if I don't know that she is on her way to work.

I don't bother to brush my teeth, but thankfully Mom doesn't seem to notice.

The sky is winter blue and the air is crisp and more than chilly but less than cold. There's frost on the windshield. I think it looks like lace. I run my fingers over it and they hurt from the iciness.

"Looks like lace, doesn't it?" Mom observes, surprising me while the two of us wait for the defroster to melt the frost.

"That's exactly what I was thinking!"

She wraps her pinky around mine. "You owe me a Coke," she says.

As we wait for the car to warm up, Mom says that Doctor Morgenstern reminded her that grief gets worse around the holidays. "And here we are with Thanksgiving next week and Christmas on its way and it is so easy to get sad," she says.

I don't say anything but it makes me feel better that maybe there's an actual psychological reason for this.

"Do you know what a mantilla is?" Mom asks. "It's a beautiful lace veil that women wore in Spain. The colors were significant. White for weddings. And maybe bullfights? And black—"

"For funerals," I say.

"Well, no. I mean, maybe. But traditionally a woman wore a black mantilla if she had an audience with the pope."

The defroster has defrosted and the windshield sparkles with water. Mom turns on the windshield wipers and we both sit there watching them wipe away what used to be frost that looked like lace.

"That's weird," I say as Mom backs out of the driveway. "How many women have audiences with the pope?"

"I don't know, Clementine. This was an old tradition."

She sounds impatient, and I don't blame her one bit.

I close my eyes for the rest of the ride, trying not to

wonder in what world there were enough Spanish women visiting the pope to have an official color for their veils.

—⽊—

Mom drops me off and says something cheerful and optimistic. I slink out of the car and give her a kind of half wave. As soon as the sound of her pulling away dies out, I make an about-face and walk away from the school. I don't have a plan. In fact, I didn't even know what I was going to do until I did it.

Cars keep pulling up and kids keep getting out of them and there's a crowd moving like one big blob into the school. I watch it for a minute, noticing how if I squint the blob looks like something in my chemistry textbook, something multicolored and slowly pulsating. Then, without a thought in my head, I continue in the direction that is not toward school.

A yellow school bus passes me, the faces of the kids a blur.

If I were on my way to a bullfight, I would have on a white mantilla. If I were on my way to meet the pope, I would have on a black mantilla. I imagine the scratchy feel of lace on my head and shoulders. Do mantillas cover the face? I decide they do and imagine peeking out at the world through the holes in the lace pattern. Dappled like light through the leaves on trees. Bullfight or pope? Pope. I am covered in black lace. Funeral. Surely black mantillas were worn at funerals.

Halley's funeral was like peeking out through lace. Distorted faces and broken images. So many white flowers, the smell choking me. The white coffin, smaller than the coffins for grown-ups. Mom's frightened, wild eyes. Her face looming too close to me and her voice, choked, saying, "Let's go see her and say goodbye," and I don't understand that she means we are going to see Halley, who is in that kid-size coffin in a fancy room with an Oriental rug and plush blue chairs. She is in there looking like she's made out of wax and before we get too close, I drop Mom's hand and run out of there as fast as I can. Images of men in jackets and ties, women with dark lipstick, kids from school looking terrified.

Then I'm out the door, outside, and it's raining. Not hard, but soft, like feathers brushing my cheeks. I lift my face upward and stick out my tongue and drink raindrops.

I hope this makes me feel alive. A girl standing in the rain with her tongue out, drinking raindrops, is alive, isn't she? But I feel nothing at all.

That's when it started. This feeling of nothingness.

Virginia and her mom came and got me and led me back into the funeral home. That suffocating smell of flowers. No air. Sad faces. People crying. The kid-size white coffin. Then Mom is taking my arm and we go back outside and climb into a limousine. But it's not a limousine, I realize once we are settled into the back seat. It's a hearse. I can smell the undertaker's aftershave, too spicy and too strong. Behind us, a line of cars follow.

Mom has my hand and she's holding on too tight.

"I don't get it, Clementine," she says. "Our family already had ours, right? Your dad, right?"

Somehow, I understand this to mean that because Dad died, Mom thought we were safe from more tragedy.

I nod because this is what she wants from me.

She keeps saying words but I can't take them in. They just fly around in the stale air between us.

When the car stops, I look out the window and all I see are tombstones. We are at the cemetery. We are burying

Halley. My door opens and a black gloved hand reaches in and gently helps me out.

And I stand there, people walking slowly past me, their gazes directed at the ground.

That is where I've come today.

I am standing in that spot where I stood the day of Halley's funeral, except no one else is here and she is already buried, not waiting inside her white coffin to be lowered into the ground. Without having to think, I follow the winding path that leads to her grave. I know the route by heart, know it like it's a poem I've memorized or a song I've been singing forever. I go past the family who all died of the Spanish influenza and the monument to dead soldiers and the weird bench where a woman wanted her loved ones to sit and think about her, and then I'm at Halley's.

I sink to the grass, which is damp and cold. My sweatpants immediately are wet in the knees. I pluck a few blades of grass that escaped the mower and readjust the fake orange flowers Mom left there in a vase.

Somewhere in the distance I hear weird bird noises.

"So," I say, "here we are. All the way back here."

CHAPTER TWENTY-ONE

IN WHICH A BOY APPEARS

For the rest of the week, Mom takes me to school and as soon as she drives off, I turn around and walk to the cemetery where I spend the day at Halley's grave. Surely the automated system the school has for reporting absences to parents has been calling her every evening. But Mom doesn't mention it. She just digs her keys out of her purse and cheerfully asks, "Ready?"

In the car today, she makes small talk about her latest craft project—a temperature blanket, which has a complicated system for recording the high temperature every day and matching that to a color chart, then she knits two rows in that color.

"Can you believe it's going to be sixty-eight degrees

today? In November?" she says. "That's Cumin, so there's going to be this stripe of Cumin in the middle of all that Maritime and Delft."

Mom shakes her head, like she's just discovered a new planet or something. "Who would have thought weather could be so . . . I don't know . . . interesting? Or creative?"

To me, it seems like an enormous waste of time to record a year's worth of temperatures and knit them into a blanket. Because if something terrible happens that year, you will have a reminder of the day it happened right there on your temperature blanket. I wonder what color yarn Mom would have used for the day Halley died. It was colder than sixty-eight degrees that day, so not Cumin. I keep these thoughts to myself because Mom is enjoying her temperature blanket so much.

"Look at how beautiful Pink Bliss looks next to Amethyst, Clementine," she says that night as she starts to knit her two rows of Cumin.

I force myself to nod and make a noise that sounds positive.

"You should start knitting again," Mom tells me.

"Okay," I say.

"You liked knitting hats for preemies," Mom says.

"I'll knit one tonight." Who knows? Maybe it will help with this growing feeling of hopelessness.

Mom grins at me. "That's good!"

She goes back to her Cumin rows. "There's something I want to talk to you about," she says without looking up.

"I know already," I say, because the automated attendance system has surely been calling her.

She looks up, frowning. "You do?"

"I'm sorry!" I say, and burst into tears.

Before she can say anything, I run upstairs to my room. I take out my ridiculous sparkly unicorn notebook and write: I will go to school tomorrow. I will not break mom's heart.

But then tomorrow comes and I do not go to school. I go to the cemetery intending to discuss something with Halley. Once I get there, I just kind of say hello, then I read or stare up at the sky or pluck blades of grass out and pile them up or write random stuff in my notebook.

Highest daily temperature ever recorded: 134, in Death Valley, on July 10, 1913.

What color would 134 degrees be?

Heat Wave? Red Hot metal? Rage?

And:

Synonyms for forgiveness:

absolution, mercy, grace.

Antonyms for forgiveness:

censure, mercilessness, blame.

And:

Ten most common causes of childhood deaths:

Car crash, firearm injury, cancer, suffocation, drowning, poisoning, congenital anomalies, heart disease, fire, homicide.

Sometimes I watch sad people come and go.

A car pulls up and an old, trembly man gets out, clutching a bouquet of mums. And a younger woman holds his elbow to help him navigate across the grass until they reach the grave they're looking for. Then he places the mums there—spidery, yellow and white—and the two of them stare at the ground sadly for five or ten minutes before they make their way back to the car.

A middle-aged woman arrives alone. She's dressed fancy, in a camel coat and silk scarf and practical high heels. She's holding a bonsai tree in a blue pot and she fidgets with it at the grave, placing it in front, then at either side, each time stepping back to assess how it looks there. Resigned, she moves it back to one corner, looks sadly at the ground for five or ten minutes, then leaves.

A young woman glides by on a bike, a baby wearing a tiny pink bike helmet in a seat on the back. The woman has on one of those thick, woolly South American sweaters and wire-rimmed glasses and she leaves something too small for me to make out on a grave. She tenderly runs her fingers over the pink marble, then hops back on her bike and rides off.

The old man is visiting his wife with his daughter. The middle-aged woman is visiting her husband. The young woman is visiting her daughter who died as a little baby.

And I am visiting my sister. I wonder if any of them noticed me, the girl stretched out on a grave writing in a notebook. I wonder why they thought I was here, who *I* was visiting. I wonder if they feel the same way I do, and that's why they came.

⸙

"I thought I might find you here," a slightly out-of-breath voice says.

I look up, and walking toward me is Jude Banks, the kid from City of Angels who I came to this very spot with once last year. The kid I wrote that letter to from Sandy Point. A flash of the letter he wrote back to me, still in its envelope, unopened, on the front table where we put our keys and stuff, pops into my mind.

"Jude Banks," I say.

"Clementine Marsh," he says, standing beside me now.

Jude sits down beside me, and I see immediately

that in just a year he's grown up some. Less boy, more teenager.

"You never answered my letter," he says.

"I never opened your letter," I admit. I don't tell him that I forgot about it.

"This place where you were? When you wrote it?"

"Sandy Point."

"Was it like Strawberry Fields?" He looks down, embarrassed for me.

I shake my head. "It's more like one of those schools parents send uncontrollable kids to."

He looks back up at that and grins. "Weren't you always uncontrollable?"

"Funny," I say as I throw some of the grass I've been plucking at him.

"Dear Clementine," he says, "even though your letter made me laugh—a lot—I'm sorry to hear that you're at this place. Sounds pretty awful. Plus, why do you like doing laundry? That's the most boring chore ever."

"Is that all of it?"

"More or less."

I think of me standing in that laundry room with my

face pressed against the warmth of the dryer and realize that was the only place I was getting any warmth or even contact. Pathetic.

"I called to see if you were back home and your mother told me you weren't at school—" Jude begins.

"She said that?"

He nods. "But she doesn't know where you go. I figured that out on my own."

"Smart guy."

Jude blushes a little. After a pause, he says, "You come here every day?"

"Yup."

He nods again.

"Do you talk to your dad, too?" Jude asks, motioning toward the grave right next to Halley's. There are gold and orange chrysanthemums in a planter there. I guess Mom leaves flowers at both.

"No. I don't really know him."

Then we just sit in silence. Overhead, a formation of Canadian geese flies past, looking like air force stunt flyers in formation. I wonder how they know to do that? How do they know where they fit into that V?

"Funny how they each know their place, isn't it?" Jude says. "Like no one tries to overtake the bird in front of them and no one lags behind."

I don't tell him that he just said exactly what I was thinking, but I smile because he did.

"Jude, why are you cutting school?"

"I'm not. It's Teacher Professional Day. Whatever that is. I told you about it in my letter. I also asked you if you wanted to meet up."

"Ah. The letter."

"I didn't tell your mother where you were," Jude says. "In case you were wondering."

It probably doesn't matter if she knows since she's kept up the ruse of taking me to school every day without saying a word. But still I say, "Thanks."

Jude is plucking grass now and adding it to what's left of my pile.

"Do you want to go see Katie?" I ask him after a while.

He shakes his head. "I'm trying not to be sad," he says.

Of course, going to Katie's grave makes him sad, I realize. He adored her.

"We got a puppy," Jude says after a little more silence. "A mini-Aussiedoodle. Edie. She's a genius."

I laugh. "Of course she is."

"Do you want to see a picture?"

Jude takes out his phone and scrolls through it, then holds it out for me to see Edie's adorable white-and-gray face, tilted to one side in a quizzical expression.

"She looks like a genius," I say.

He scrolls to another picture of her and I secretly hope this is the last one.

In this picture she has a lime-green Frisbee in her mouth.

"Cute," I say. And she is.

Thankfully, he puts the phone back in his pocket.

"My parents thought it was a good idea. So I wouldn't be lonely."

"Did it work?"

Jude shakes his head. "But I think it helps my mom."

"Are you lonely?" I ask him, even though I know the answer.

"Lonely for Katie," he says. He looks right at me. "But I guess I will be forever."

I open my mouth, as if I'm going to tell him something, too. But the words don't come out. They just stay lodged deep in my chest. So deep that I'm not sure they'll ever come out. I think of buried treasures lying on the ocean floor, undiscovered. I think of the lost city of Atlantis, how it was maybe buried in mud for thousands of years. I think of all the things that are buried and lost but valuable. Important. Like my words.

CHAPTER TWENTY-TWO

IN WHICH I AM ORANGE AND LIME GREEN AND CHARTREUSE

The next morning, I come downstairs dressed like I'm going to school—the black-and-tan plaid pants that are kind of bell-bottoms but only come up to my ankles that I bought at the one vintage clothing store here before Halley died, a faded pink sweater that I've had since I used to wear pink a lot, and a knit orange hat that I got at Urban Outfitters, also before Halley died. I found all these treasures last night when I couldn't sleep and decided to rummage through my closet and drawers, in hopes of finding a way to reinvent myself. Sometime between leaving Jude at the cemetery and going to bed, I decided that reinventing myself was maybe a way out of this place I'm stuck in.

Mom frowns at me when I sit down in front of my toasted frozen waffle. She's added two microwaved breakfast sausages this morning. I take them off the plate and put them on my napkin.

"I'm vegetarian," I say. "Or maybe vegan." (Note to self: Look up the difference between vegetarian and vegan.)

"Since when? And also, what are you wearing?"

"Since yesterday," I tell her.

"You have on orange and pink," Mom points out. "Which only look good together in flowers. Like tulips. Or zinnias."

I don't answer. I just suck the fake maple syrup off the piece of waffle in my mouth until the waffle is emptied and tastes just like cardboard. Then I swallow that and repeat with the next piece.

"Well, I already started chili in the slow cooker so become a vegetarian tomorrow, okay?" Mom says, grabbing her keys and jingling them in the vicinity of my face. "Let's go."

I get up and put on the pièce de résistance, my father's old brown corduroy jacket. It's faded and frayed at the cuffs, the only thing of his I have. Halley kept all sorts of his stuff in her room—pictures and his watch and a pair of his jeans and an old bottle cap collection from when he was a kid, plus who knows what else. But I just took this when Mom finally cleaned out his side of the closet, which was years after he died. I used to find it creepy how all his shirts and pants hung there, waiting for someone who was never coming back. I picked this from the pile Mom had on the bed because I thought I could smell him on it. Which is ridiculous because smells fade after a few years. But even as I put it on this morning, I catch a whiff of him, tobacco and sweat and the outdoors.

"Ready," I say.

She studies me a bit longer, then nods like she's decided something and heads toward the door. I follow the back of her coat, which is an ugly red wool one that she bought after she took a test in a magazine to find out what season she was. Then you dress in the colors of that season. She's a winter apparently, so she should wear holly-berry red, emerald green, cobalt blue, black, and white. I think the coat was the only thing she bought according to her season, and really, it does not look good.

But for some reason, in the car I say, "Remember when

we all took the test to see what season we were?"

And just like that, memories of that night tumble through me. The three of us in our pajamas reading Mom's magazines, and Mom deciding we should take the test "What Color Season Am I?" She got paper and pens and Halley and I sat on the floor at her feet as she read us the questions. The catch was that you took the quiz for each other, so Halley did me and I did her and we both did Mom.

"Does this person look healthy and alive in true white, as opposed to ivory or off-white?"

"Does this person look healthy and alive in blue-gray?"

I rolled my eyes. "No, she looks one hundred percent dead in blue-gray," I said.

Halley punched my arm. "Stop it! Don't say I look dead. It freaks me out."

"This question is better," Mom said. "Is she overwhelmed by pure black?"

I wonder if Mom remembers Halley saying that? If she remembers that when the question was, "Does this person look healthy and alive in pumpkin orange?" Halley started to cry?

But Mom is smiling that sad memory-of-Halley smile.

"You were an autumn and she was a spring," Mom says. "Funny. I don't remember what I was."

"Winter. That's why you bought the holly-berry-red coat."

"Ugh. I hate this coat. It's so . . . red."

We both laugh. Then I tell her that autumns are supposed to wear orange.

"You mocked my hat," I say, "but it is in my season."

Mom doesn't answer. I can see that she's gone off somewhere else, somewhere that Halley's in. For the rest of the ride, I pick at the loose threads of Dad's cuff and Mom hangs out with Halley.

We get to school and when Mom tells me to have a good day, I look at her hard. She knows I haven't been to school in three days. Why does she keep pretending? Why isn't she mad at me? Why doesn't she say something?

"Clementine, I have to open the store this morning," is all she says, and she makes a shooing motion with her hands.

After I get out of the car, I stand there with all the kids going to school rushing past me. Stay or go? I want mostly to go, but didn't I reinvent myself? I'm a person who wears an orange hat and vintage pants. I'm a vegetarian, or maybe even a vegan.

"Hey, nice hat, Pamplemousse," I hear, and I turn, and Miles is standing there in a navy peacoat, which looks good. I guess it matches Miles's season. *Does this person look healthy and alive in navy blue*? As soon as I think this an image of Halley, dead, jumps in front of me. Blue-gray. Her whole body was blue-gray.

I start to walk away from the school, but Miles has come up beside me as if I'm not going in the wrong direction. "Have you started reading *The Kite Runner*? It's about a million pages long."

Just like that I'm now going toward the school, Miles talking on and on about Amir and Kabul and a bunch of other things I don't understand.

Sometimes, like this morning, my brain gets stuck and I can't unstick it. I can't stop thinking about that stupid "What Color Season Am I?" quiz, and when I do I see Halley blue-gray. *Does this person look healthy and alive in deep burgundy? Does this person look healthy and alive in light mango?*

To try and stop it, I turn my attention to Miles. Are

they a spring or a summer? Do they look healthy and alive in navy blue?

Blue-gray Halley threatens to appear, so I push hard on my eyelids. Am I breathing fast and shallow? Am I about to have a panic attack? Again? Right here in English class?

"Pop quiz," Ms. Quigley is saying. She says, "Easy," and "Just one question," and then she's writing on the board in her big, loopy handwriting: *What does the kite symbolize in* The Kite Runner?

Everyone starts writing right away, because they have been reading the book for the past five days. I try to remember what Miles was saying about Amir and Kabul, but all I can think is, *Does this person look healthy and alive in bright yellow-green?*

Think of kites, I order myself. Think of Kabul, which is possibly in Afghanistan.

I watch Lacy and Casey, both writing furiously.

I close my eyes and force an image of a kite to show up, to push away blue-gray Halley. That day at the hospital, I shouldn't have stared so hard because now all I can see is the way it was all dark blue and gray around her ankles.

Kites!

I hear myself breathing and wonder if everyone else hears me, too.

Kites.

I try to steady my breathing.

I write: *In* The Kite Runner, *kites symbolize freedom. And happiness. Amir was happy when he flew a kite.*

I pause to wonder what *The Kite Runner* is about. A boy named Amir in Kabul, obviously. Did Miles say something about a friend?

Does this person look healthy and alive with dark blue and gray spots around their ankles?

A nurse touched my arm that day when she saw me staring like that. "It's okay," she said softly. "That's because there's no blood flow anymore."

I looked at her horrified because like two hours ago Halley's blood was flowing and her skin was lovely and she was laughing with Celeste and walking into the cafeteria.

My hand is shaking, but I manage to write, *But the kite also signifies guilt because of Amir's friend.*

The next day in English, Ms. Quigley hands back the pop quizzes. She places mine facedown on my desk and says, "This would have been an A if you'd only said a bit more."

I turn the paper over. There's a red B at the top and beside it Ms. Quigley wrote: *Talk to me about Amir's guilt over Hassan!!!!!*

Not bad, I think. I got a B without even reading any of the book all because of Amir's guilt. And Miles being my friend and telling me about him.

CHAPTER TWENTY-THREE

IN WHICH I PAY THE PIPER

The reinvented me goes to school the next day in brown corduroy overalls that are way too short for me with a long-sleeved thermal undershirt underneath, and my orange knit hat. I decide that tomorrow, which is Saturday, I will go to the only vintage clothing store in town and buy clothes that fit the new me. Maybe I will also get a skateboard. A long time ago, Halley and me and Virginia and Celeste made skateboards out of pieces of wood that we painted, attached to old roller skates. I painted mine purple and named it the People Eater. That thing is probably still in the basement, but I want something sleek and new. Maybe I'll even skateboard to school, I decide.

I fantasize about this in homeroom, which is really

like a holding cell for us while a teacher takes attendance and we listen to morning announcements read by the principal's secretary, Mrs. Fishe, in her thick New Jersey accent. It's like one of the Sopranos is telling us what's for hot lunch and which after-school activities are canceled. Today it's fish sticks and mashed potatoes and there's no Chess Club. But I'm only half listening as I imagine myself gliding down hills on a new skateboard, my orange hat bobbing in the wind.

"Ms. Marsh?" the homeroom teacher is saying like she's said it once already.

She's pointing with her too-long, too-red fingernails at the intercom on the wall where Mrs. Fishe's voice is saying, "Clementine Marsh, please come to the office."

Of course, everyone is staring at me.

I get up and walk out, pretending I'm already on that skateboard. Someone giggles but I just keep gliding out the door, down the hall, and down the stairs to the office.

Mrs. Fishe pounces on me as soon as I walk in. "Mr. Lombardo needs to see you. Take a seat over there until he comes for you." *Lom-bah-do,* she says. *Ovah dere.*

I go to the row of three seats outside Mr. Lombardo's office and sit down, wondering what he is going to do with me. Cutting school is a serious offense, and since I already have a record, I'm worried he might suspend me. Mr. Lombardo isn't the principal, he's the *vice* principal, which means he's the one who's in charge of disciplinary action. But I have no idea how Mr. Lombardo works. Mom convinced him to just give me detention for the Lacy/Casey thing, so maybe there's hope.

I'm so wrapped up in my own thoughts that I don't even realize that Samantha is sitting across from me until she says in a stage whisper, "What did *you* do?" Her big blue eyes are round and practically spinning.

I shrug. "No idea. You?"

"Ms. Quigley caught me smoking in the bathroom. But they don't count because they were *clove* cigarettes, which aren't even real cigarettes," Samantha says passionately.

"Right," I say.

"See? Obvious!"

I hear footsteps and look away from Samantha and up toward them, right at my mother's angry face.

"They called you?" I say.

"Mr. Lombardi—"

"Lombardo," Samantha corrects cheerfully. "I got caught smoking *clove* cigarettes. They're not even real!"

Before I can protest even more, Mr. Lombardo's office door opens, and he steps out.

"I don't think we're going to be so lucky this time," Mom whispers to me.

Mr. Lombardo used to be a gym teacher and he still wears tracksuits or sweatpants and T-shirts with sneakers every day. He has a buzz cut and a square jaw and he always looks mad, like his team just lost.

"Marsh," he says into the space between Samantha, Mom, and me.

I get up, fast. The guy terrifies me.

"And Mrs. Marsh," he adds, leading us both inside to his trophy-cluttered office.

"Mr. Lombardo," Mom says, "you know that Clementine has been going through a lot."

"I'm going to cut to the chase, Mrs. Marsh. I don't waste working parents' time," Mr. Lombardo says.

I'm still standing, because Mom is. But he's sitting

at his desk, and he leans back in his chair with his hands behind his head and says, real casually, "Clementine is expelled until the Monday after Thanksgiving."

"Expelled!" Mom says.

"Yup," Mr. Lombardo says. "For truancy."

My heart, which had been banging against my ribs, seems to drop all the way to my knees. Truancy. I have no defense. I am a truant.

"But shouldn't she get a warning or something first? A second chance maybe?" Mom says. "Detention?"

"According to the school handbook, truancy gets you suspension. Now I understand she's having problems adjusting—"

"It's not just that," Mom says in a low voice.

Mr. Lombardo looks about as uncomfortable as a person can look. He shuffles some papers on his very messy desk and pulls out from the mess some brochures, which he hands to me without looking at me.

WHAT TO DO IF YOU'RE SAD, one says.

1-800-GET-HELP, another one says.

To my surprise, the third one is for City of Angels.

"Some resources," Mr. Lombardo says, still not looking

at me. Or Mom. "And Mrs. O'Malley, in Guidance, is always here to talk. You can stop by there any time." He finally looks up at me. "You've got to pay the piper, you know what I'm saying, Clementine?"

Mom tries again to get me a reduced sentence. "It's my fault, too," she says, but Mr. Lombardo tells her parents always try to take the blame for their kids, which isn't a good thing to do.

"You think you're helping Clementine by saying it's your fault," he says, "but you're not."

I stop listening. In my head, I'm hearing Halley sing "The Twelve Days of Christmas" in order, even the ones after five golden rings.

" 'On the eleventh day of Christmas my true love sent to me, eleven pipers piping,'" she sang in her high, sweet voice, "'ten lords a-leaping' . . ."

Then I'd start singing louder and out of order. "'Nine maids a-milking, eight lords a-leaping'—"

"That's not how it goes!" she'd yell, and then she would start crying and I would get in trouble.

Like now. Eleven pipers piping and I'm paying every one of them.

CHAPTER TWENTY-FOUR

IN WHICH I SPELUNK

On Day Three of my expulsion, I knock on Mom's bedroom door after she gets home from work.

When she calls "Come in," and I step inside, she's sitting on her bed, phone in hand, giggling and flushed.

"Do you need something, sweetie?" she asks me. Despite the *sweetie*, she sounds impatient.

"We can talk when you're off the phone."

"Great!" she says to me. "I'm back," she says into the phone.

I want to leave but my feet feel like they are Gorilla Glued to the floor.

Mom realizes I'm still there and says, "We'll talk later, Clementine, okay?"

"Who are you talking to?" I ask her.

"A friend," she says, shaking her head. "I don't know," she says to her friend, "my daughter is looming about."

"I'm not looming," I say with my righteous indignation.

She gives me her impatient face and I somehow pull my right foot off the floor, and then the left one, and manage to slowly make my way out the door, where I stand, confused. I press my ear to the door, but all I can hear is low murmuring and a few intermittent giggles. What is going on in there? I decide I will wait right here and find out. So I slide down the door to the floor and sit there. When Mom comes out, she will find me right here, waiting.

Except no one can sit on a floor for as long as she is on that phone. One hour, then another, and still the murmuring and giggles with no sign of her coming out.

I give up and go back to my room and pick up my phone for the first time since I got expelled. I was too embarrassed to talk to anybody. I find a text message from Samantha:

3 day suspension. U?

I realize the message came three days ago, the very afternoon we saw Mr. Lombardo.

There's a more recent message from Miles:

Whereforth art thou, pamplemousse???

And a real surprise. A message from Jayden.

Hey. What's up? Wanna hang?

For some reason, the texts exhaust me. Or maybe Mom's strange behavior exhausts me. But I practically crawl into bed and bury myself under my blankets and pillows until Mom comes in, finally off her call.

She sits beside me on the bed and says, "So," and then nothing else.

I get a strange feeling in my stomach, the kind I get when I'm about to hear bad news.

"So?" I say.

"The friend on the phone?"

"Uh-huh," I say, not actually wanting her to say whatever she's about to say.

"His name is George."

"Okay."

"I met him at the store. He's actually a knitter, and he comes in quite a bit. He's making a temperature blanket, too," she says.

"Okay," I say again, even though nothing about this feels okay.

"I've been trying to talk to you about this for weeks," she says. "Girl talk, remember?"

I do remember, but I don't say anything. I just feel that strange feeling in my stomach growing.

"I like him. A lot," Mom says. "And he likes me. A lot."

"Okay," I say, wondering how many times I can say okay.

"We have lunch together almost every day. There's this new bistro near the store called Paris Café and we go there and we have moules frites—"

"Mules? What?"

"Mussels," Mom says. "Or roast chicken or . . . why

am I telling you what we have for lunch?" she says, and shakes her head. "I'm just so nervous. What I mean to say is I think he's maybe my boyfriend—"

"You don't have boyfriends," I practically shout.

"I know. Your father died a long time ago, and I think I've gone on three dates in all this time—"

"You went on three dates? When?"

"Like every three or four years I'd go out with someone once, and then I'd feel guilty and not go on a second date. But, Clementine, I'm sad and I'm lonely and this man, George, is a nice man and—"

"George is an old-guy name," I say.

"It is not!" Mom says, but she laughs when she says it. "I've invited him for Thanksgiving. So you can meet him."

"He's coming here? On an official holiday?"

"Sweetie—"

"Go away!" I yell.

She hesitates, but then I say it again. "Go away!"

When she leaves, I imagine I'm in a cave, a place I would never actually go because caves freak me out. They are like a hundred thousand years old, maybe even older, and thinking about that much time makes me hyperventilate because, for example, where are all the people who have died in all these years? Literally, where are their bodies? There isn't room for a hundred thousand years of dead bodies, is there?

Also, millions of bats live in caves. Millions. Once I was sleeping over at Virginia's and we were in bed and a bat swooped right over our heads and we screamed so loud and hard that her mother almost fell trying to get to us. When she saw there was a bat in the room, she started screaming, too, and then she ran to get a broom but what good is a broom against a bat? Against a million bats?

Some people, like Halley, think stalagmites and stalactites are beautiful, but I think they are creepy because they're formed from cave water dripping and where is that water even coming from? Plus, they're sharp and pointy like icicles, like swords, like spears.

Despite these things, this afternoon under my blankets and pillows, with all sounds muffled and darkness all around me, I pretend I am in a cave, and I am peaceful there, not terrified. There's something called total cave darkness, which is exactly what it sounds like, and after two days in total cave darkness a person actually loses her mind. How do I know this? Halley was obsessed with caves. She did a science project on some famous cave in Borneo, the one with a million bats in it, and she built a model of it out of papier-mâché with melted crayon stalagmites and stalactites and origami bats. I thought she was just being weird, but today I kind of understand her fascination.

I don't know how long I stay in my metaphorical cave, not thinking or seeing or hearing anything. At one point I wonder if this is what it feels like to be dead. At another point I wonder if this is what it feels like to be alive. And then Mom is poking at me and telling me to get up because how can I breathe like that?

I stay in my cave.

In my cave, Samantha doesn't want to be my friend and Jayden doesn't want to hang out and Miles isn't quoting Shakespeare and there's no George and Halley isn't dead. There are no bats in my cave. No peanut allergies.

There is nothing but me.

When I emerge, it's the middle of the night. I look out the window and see snow flurries in the light of the streetlight. There's frost on cars and tree branches and the world looks so beautiful that I want to be in it. Not the actual world, but this middle-of-the-night world with its frost and snow flurries and cloudy sky.

Down the stairs and out the door and it isn't until I'm standing in the street with the snow wetting my hair that I realize two things. One: I don't have a coat on. And two: I don't have a key to get back in the house. I decide to not let these things bother me yet. Instead, I catch snowflakes with my tongue and close my eyes and open my arms and start to spin very, very slowly.

I wonder: Can I get covered in frost, too? Encased in lacy ice? I'd be in my own snow globe, safe. I spin a little faster, the street slippery beneath my feet.

"What are you doing out here?" Mom's voice cuts through the beautiful world, bringing me slamming back into the real one.

She's wrapped in her ratty bathrobe and her hair is all messy with bed head and she's standing at the end of the driveway, her eyes frightened.

"It's three o'clock in the morning," she says.

I have stopped spinning but my arms are still opened, and I feel awkward and ridiculous and wet.

"You are going to catch pneumonia," she says, sliding her way over to me and grabbing my arm and pulling me with her back inside.

As soon as the warmth of the house hits me, I start to shiver. Mom wraps the scratchy afghan that someone crocheted for her years ago around me and urges me onto the couch.

"I'll make you hot chocolate," she says. "Don't move. Do you hear me?"

I don't answer because my teeth are chattering.

In no time she's back with a cup of instant cocoa, the kind with the fake marshmallows, which is my favorite kind.

"What were you thinking?" Mom asks me wearily. She sinks onto the couch beside me. "Just tell me what you were thinking."

The cocoa is hot, and I burn my tongue, but I don't even care. What was I thinking? About caves and bats and frost and snow. But if I tell her that, she'll think I'm lost again. And maybe I am.

Mom rubs my arms to help warm me up and it feels nice.

Maybe a long time passes, maybe a medium time, but Mom says finally, "Let's go to bed, okay?"

But I don't. I just sit on the couch under the ugly, scratchy afghan, and watch the sky outside slowly start to brighten. The snow has stopped. The streets and cars and everything out there are covered with a fine layer of it, like dust or powder, that sparkles as the sun comes out. I wish I thought the world looked beautiful, like I did a few hours ago. But honestly, it doesn't even look familiar.

CHAPTER TWENTY-FIVE

IN WHICH I DISCOVER THE JOY OF BAKING

Thanksgiving is two days away and I have nothing to do but ignore Miles, Jayden, and Samantha and try to keep dark thoughts away. The first is easy: Turn off phone. The second is harder, especially at night. But days aren't much better. Mom is at work and eating lunch with George and I'm here with the noises of the house and my mind tossing around in my head. Like a ship in a storm, I think, and immediately write that down in my notebook under the heading: *Bad Metaphors and Similes.*

I find myself thinking about Gloria from City of Angels and how she taught us to knit because keeping busy held sad thoughts at bay. Mom has commandeered all the yarn in the house for her temperature blanket, so knitting isn't an option. I remember the comfort of doing the laundry at Sandy Point, but when I go down to the basement, I see that Mom has washed, dried, and folded all our laundry already. Getting back in bed is starting to look very appealing. Just as I head back upstairs, though, the phone is ringing. I think we are the last people in America who still have a landline, because Mom thinks if there's ever a tornado or some other natural disaster the landline will still work and our cell phones won't. Which doesn't make sense. Wouldn't it be the other way around? Also, we don't get tornadoes in our part of the country.

"Hello?" I say into the phone.

"Clementine!" I hear, and immediately recognize Virginia's mother's voice. It feels like a hug. "Is your mom there, hon?"

"She's at work," I say, even though for all I know she's eating moules frites with her boyfriend.

"Work?"

"At Forget-Me-Knot. She has mother's hours."

"Huh," she says. "Okay. Hey! Why aren't you in school?"

"Thanksgiving," I say vaguely.

"Geez, don't tell Virginia. She goes all the way through Wednesday."

"I won't," I say, as if I ever talk to Virginia.

"Here's the thing. Jack's mother has taken a bad fall and he has to go down to West Palm Beach and be with her. Bad timing, right? Right before Thanksgiving?"

I mumble something that I hope sounds like an agreement.

"So, I was thinking the girls and I would just come to you guys for the holiday. We'll get an Airbnb or something because there's so many of us. Plus, I am enormous with this baby. Honestly, I hope I fit through the door."

"Ha-ha," I manage.

"Won't that be fun, though, Clementine? Just like the old days?"

"Just like the old days," I say.

Except you're pregnant again, you have a baby and a husband, and Halley's dead.

"Can you fill your mom in and have her call me when she gets home? Geez," she says again, and I can practically hear her shaking her head, "I had no idea she had a job."

"She gets a big discount on yarn and stuff."

She drops her voice. "I think it's really wonderful that she gets out of the house every day. And is among people."

For a moment, I think she means out of the house and away from me. But then I realize she means because of Halley.

Her voice brightens. "Tell her I am absolutely craving pie. All kinds of pie. Jack has been making apple pies like there's no tomorrow."

"I'll tell her," I say. "Pies."

After I hang up, I lie on the couch and let all the things Virginia's mom said cover me like a lead blanket. Three more people coming for Thanksgiving. Four, if you count Poppy. She is enormous and won't fit through the door. Mom is among people. Jack has been making apple pies like there's no tomorrow.

Like there's no tomorrow.

What a weird thing to say.

We don't know when there's no tomorrow for us. A tornado could hit the house and leave only the landline still breathing. There're drunk drivers and peanut butter and Advil. So many things that take away tomorrows.

But the more I think about *like there's no tomorrow*,

the more I start to understand that it's maybe actually a good thing to say. Have fun! Eat moules frites! Make pies! With abandon! And joy!

That's when I decide that I will, like Jack, make pies like there's no tomorrow. There have to be pies on Thanksgiving. Pumpkin, for sure. The aforementioned apple. Long ago, at my grandmother's, she had something called mincemeat pie. She said it was traditional. So pumpkin, apple, mincemeat . . . key lime? Lemon meringue? Pecan? All of the above?

I spend the morning watching YouTube videos of how to make a pie. First thing I learn: In order to make pie, you need to make pie *crust*. According to the nine YouTube videos I watch, pie crust should be tender and flaky, flaky and buttery, buttery and tender. You might have pie anxiety. But! You are excited about this! The people making pie crusts are in their own kitchens, or in kitchens that look like chemistry labs; they are wearing scrubs, or colorful aprons, or clothes that match their appliances; they tell me that I can use a pastry cutter or a blender or my fingers to make pie crust; they call me friend, viewer, fellow baker.

With all of this information and my mother's dog-eared copy of *The Silver Palate Cookbook*, I go into the kitchen and line the flour and sugar and salt and butter on the counter. I have no idea what *shortening* is, but most people don't use it, anyway. *The Silver Palate* says to use lard, but I'm not exactly sure what that is, either, and I doubt that Mom has any. So I just grab all the butter in the fridge. Then I set to work.

After I add all the dry ingredients, I add chopped-up butter and use my fingers to smoosh it. The mixture has to be *the size of peas* or *as big as walnuts* or *resembles coarse meal*. Peas, I know. Also, walnuts. Coarse meal? No idea. I settle on somewhere between peas and walnuts, add the ice water by tablespoons, and eventually get something like dough that kind of holds together. I *don't handle it too much* and *use the heel of my hand* and *make two discs*. Except I make eight discs because I am going to make a lot of pies.

By the time Mom gets home at three, six of my pies are waiting to be filled. I found a can of cherries, so I've made one cherry pie, but I need pecans and apples and pumpkin. Mincemeat is off the list because I've never heard of most of the ingredients, like currants and sultana raisins. I also need more pie tins. The cherry pie is cooling and the empty shells are all pale and hopefully tender and flaky and buttery.

Mom surveys the kitchen (a mess) and the pie-covered counter before she even takes off her coat.

"You've been . . . baking," she says finally. "A lot!"

"Pies," I say.

"Yes, yes, I see that. They're beautiful, Clementine. But, well, there's a lot of them."

"For Thanksgiving," I say. Then I realize she doesn't know yet that Virginia and her family are coming, so I say in a big rush of words, "Virginia's mom called and Jack's mother fell or something so they're coming for Thanksgiving and staying in an Airbnb and she's super enormous and wants to eat lots of pie."

"What? They're coming here?" Mom looks so happy that I think she might burst from joy. "This is so perfect, Clementine. Isn't it?"

I almost think I can see into her brain where she's remembering last Thanksgiving and how the two of us didn't even bother with a turkey. We just got pizza and watched movies and pretended it was any old Thursday in November, and how the year before Halley was with us, and now this year there will be Virginia and her mother and Celeste and even Poppy, almost like the old days.

"It is," I say. "Almost perfect."

Mom nods and smiles. "I cannot believe you made all these pies."

I beam back at her. "Maybe I should quit school and move to Paris and go to baking school."

She laughs. "Maybe."

"Virginia's mom said to call her."

Mom finally takes off her coat and puts down her handbag and heads upstairs.

Once she's gone, I imagine heaping one of these pies with apples really high like one of the YouTube bakers did. She had on a sexy dress and jewelry and lipstick. She talked a lot about juiciness and pronounced apricots *A-pricots*. Her pie looked like a monument or a skyscraper, reaching to the sky, dusted with cinnamon sugar. I will make a pie like that, and Mom will maybe faint from the sight of such a thing of beauty.

CHAPTER TWENTY-SIX

IN WHICH GEORGE APPEARS, AND I DISAPPEAR

THANKSGIVING

Thanksgiving arrives in a torrential rain. The kind that is loud and assertive and threatening. Dark sky. Dark clouds. This is not a good omen, I think when I get out of bed. Outside my window all I can see is the wind whipping around, lifting trash-can lids and plastic bags and tossing them around. Raindrops hit the window so fast that they immediately become just a sheet of rain covering it.

Downstairs: voices.

I can make out Virginia's mom's voice and the squeals of a toddler. Why are they here so early? But then I look at my phone and see it's almost noon. I slept thirteen hours. Avoidance, maybe? Okay, definitely avoidance. George entering my life—our life—right now is not what I need.

A thought flickers across my mind like static: Will it ever be all right for a George to enter my life? To throw off the delicate balance of Mom and me and even, still, Halley?

I push that thought away. Virginia is here! I put on my orange hat but stay in my pajamas, the ones I got for Christmas a few years ago. They look like long johns and have old-fashioned station wagons with Christmas trees on their roofs all over them. I try not to think about how every year since Halley was born, Mom gave us matching pajamas at Christmas.

When I burst down the stairs, Mom says, "Clementine, you can't wear pj's all day. It's *Thanksgiving.*"

To Virginia's mom, she says, "I don't know what's up with this hat but she wears it *all the time.*"

I hug Virginia's mom, who is not enormous at all. She's adorable. She has on black leggings and a blue-and-white sweater, and her belly is a perfect hard ball between us as we hug. She smells like cookies. Or maybe just familiar.

I say how cute Poppy is, how big she's gotten in just six weeks. I half hug Celeste and big hug Virginia. Right away it strikes me as weird that she didn't run up to me as soon as I showed up. Also weird: She's wearing mascara.

Her eyelashes look kind of like spiders. But I hold on extra tight, anyway, and when I finally let go, we grin at each other.

"Why are we all still standing here?" Mom says. "Come in the kitchen and I'll put you to work." She shoots me a warning look. "While Clementine finishes getting dressed."

I consider going into the kitchen with everybody else but Virginia is already heading toward the stairs, so I follow her up.

As soon as we're in my room, she closes the door and whispers, "I have a boyfriend!"

Who is this person? I think as she gets out her phone and starts shoving pictures in my face.

Virginia narrates the photos, but real fast, so all I make out is *skiing* and *Sadie Hawkins* and *just goofing around.* The pictures fly by fast, too, but I see that in all of them a boy has his arm around Virginia's shoulder, and they are either looking at each other or she is looking at him.

"Nate," she says, sighing. "Actually, it's Nathaniel. Isn't that a fancy name? Nathaniel," she says again, like she can hardly believe it.

I cannot think of one thing to say, but I finally come up with, "Who's Sadie Hawkins?"

Virginia laughs the way a smart person tolerates someone not as smart. "Not *who*," she says. "*What*. It's a dance where the girls ask the boys to the dance instead of the other way around."

That is one of the most ridiculous things I've ever heard. What century is she living in? But I say, "Oh. Cool," even though I think the exact opposite.

"We were already boyfriend and girlfriend by then so he knew I was going to ask him, but I still showed up at his locker with a bouquet of balloons and got down on one knee and asked him. Wait. I think I have a picture."

"That's okay," I say. "I get it."

But she's already scrolling through her photos and shoving the phone back in my face. There she is, my former best friend Virginia, literally on bended knee, a bouquet of balloons floating above her head and a boy—he of the fancy name, I suppose—grinning down at her.

"My friend Cecily took the picture," she says.

She points to a face in the small crowd around them.

"Cecily," I say.

"Doesn't that practically sound French?"

"I guess?"

"Wait. I have a really cute picture of her from the hayride." She's scrolling again.

"I have to get dressed or Mom is going to be furious," I mumble, and go and stare into my closet, wondering who this person is pretending to be Virginia. When I saw her in October, she didn't seem to be my same Virginia. In just six weeks, she's changed again. I feel like there's a stranger in my room wearing too much mascara and talking like she's in a bad teen movie.

I put on the plaid pants again, but with a tee with Ruth Bader Ginsburg on it, my last gift ever from Halley. I had no feelings about RBG so I thought the gift was impersonal, like giving someone a candle or socks. So I didn't wear it, at least not until after she died.

"We should go help," I say once I'm dressed.

"Why do you wear that hat? In the house?" Virginia says.

"It's a style thing," I say.

She appears to be texting someone. "It is?"

"Are you coming?" I say from halfway out the door.

"In a minute," she says without looking up, thumbs typing like mad. "I'm just filling Cecily in."

"Okay," I say, although the whole way to the kitchen all I can think about is what she's filling Cecily in about. Me? My hat?

A text bubble appears in my mind: *She is weirder than ever!!!*

I close my eyes tight until the text bubble disappears, then I walk in the kitchen where a mostly bald man in a suit and tie is opening a bottle of wine.

Actually, there's a lot going on in the kitchen. Poppy is walking in the jerky way toddlers walk, as if she might fall facedown at any second. She's clutching one of the weird bananas I made in craft class at Sandy Point in one hand and a bottle of milk in the other.

Celeste is peeling potatoes so slowly that I don't think we will have mashed potatoes with our turkey because no way is she finishing anytime soon.

Virginia's mom is rubbing her stomach like a genie might pop out, and she's nodding and looking fascinated... but by what?

Mom looks up from basting the turkey, her face

shiny and flushed from the warmth of the oven, and says, "Clementine, this is George!" in a voice that sounds like she's telling me I just won something. The turkey baster is dripping turkey juice everywhere, including on Mom's apron, but she just stands there proudly, her hair blow-dried and pretty, her lips glossy.

George takes my hand in his weirdly buttery-soft one and kind of shakes, kind of pats it.

"I'm so happy to meet you finally," he says.

Finally?

"Your mom says you love knitting, too?"

"Not exactly," I mumble. My hand, rougher than his, is now also clammy.

"Well, I brought my temperature blanket so you can see it. Your mom told me you've really taken an interest in hers."

"Cumin," I manage. "She's using a lot of Cumin."

George gives me a big smile. "Wait until you see the different color palettes we're using!"

"Great," I say.

My head is swimming so much that I have to sit down. There's a man in our house. A man dating Mom. I almost trip over Poppy, who has abandoned walking and is instead sitting on her butt collecting crumbs. The phone is ringing, adding to all the noise of all these people. At the kitchen table, which is covered in Thanksgiving food in various stages of preparation—jellied cranberry sauce glistening from the good silver bowl, green beans that need to be microwaved and topped with sliced almonds, rolls waiting to be warmed, a Waldorf salad, and sweet potatoes topped with marshmallows and pecans—I sit down and try to stop the thoughts that are tornado-ing through my brain.

"Listen to that rain!" Virginia's mom says, making me realize no one is paying any attention to me.

I've got to get out of here. Not in the vague future. Not metaphorically. I've got to get out of here *right now*.

"Clementine," Mom is saying, "Miles is on the phone?"

"Is that your *boyfriend*?" Virginia says as I push past her. "Miles is such a cool name."

"Oh my! Look at all these pies!" Virginia's mom is saying to George. "Apparently Clementine made them all . . ."

Their voices fade as I leave the kitchen and walk out the door, into the torrential rain and wind. Branches have come off trees and are in the street. By the time I'm at the end of the driveway, I'm soaked. That's how hard it's raining. I hesitate, looking left and right, trying to decide what to do, which way to go.

But before I make up my mind, Mom is right beside me, pulling me hard toward the house.

"You can stop this, Clementine. Come on inside."

I'm so wet that my arm is slippery, and her hand keeps sliding off it.

"Talk to me, sweetie," she says.

I see she didn't grab her raincoat, either, and her beautiful hair, so full and shiny minutes ago, is already flattened and wet.

"Your hair," I say. "It looked so nice, and I ruined it."

Mom puts her hands on my shoulders and turns me so that I'm facing her.

"Listen to me. You haven't ruined anything. Not my hair or my life or . . . or Halley's."

We are both so wet that she probably doesn't even notice that I've started crying.

"I hate George," I tell her, and she pulls me close, and our soaked bodies smoosh together.

"I know, sweetie," she whispers.

"I hate Virginia."

Mom says, "Those eyelashes. Am I right?"

How dare she make me laugh? I wiggle free of her and stand there dripping.

"Inside," she says. "Shower. Warm clothes. Both of us. What do you say?"

I don't say anything. I just follow her back inside.

Virginia is standing wide-eyed in the kitchen doorway.

"Go text Cecily!" I scream at her. "Tell her that I went outside in a storm! Tell her that my mind is about to explode!"

Mom is pulling at me again, this time toward the stairs.

"Go. Now," she whispers.

I slip slide up the stairs, my bare feet so wet I can't grip tight.

In the dim light of my room, I throw my soaked body down on the bed.

The windows rattle. The rain pounds against the roof. The wind screams. But somehow none of it drowns out the noise in my head.

CHAPTER TWENTY-SEVEN

IN WHICH I ATTEMPT TO BEAT THE GUINNESS WORLD RECORD FOR PIE EATING

THANKSGIVING

I do not go down for dinner, of course. I stay in my bed in my wet clothes and try to shut off my brain. Every now and then words float up to me from the dining room where everyone else is sitting and eating turkey and mashed potatoes, et cetera. *Temperamental* floats up. And *long-term insurance*. And *gravy*. I let them swirl above me, like smoke.

Mom did appear in my doorway before dinner started and said, "Please come down for dinner, sweetie. It's Thanksgiving."

I managed to lift my head and look at her sideways. She had blow-dried her hair again and looked as pretty as before. Seeing her made my heart break because I had ruined everything for her today.

"I'm too embarrassed," I mumble.

Mom told me how everyone understood and there was nothing to be embarrassed about, but I stopped listening. I worked hard on making my mind go blank. I imagined a whiteboard in my head, covered with so many words, overlapping and smudging. I imagined picking up a dry eraser and slowly and methodically wiping the board clean. Even the shadows of blue left behind. Wiped clean. When I finished, I peeked out and Mom was gone.

The chatter downstairs seems to go on for years and years. At one point, Poppy screams for a good long while, then a brief bit of silence, then chatter again. *Nathaniel* floats up to me. And *snowflake dance*. And *stuffed*.

I start to think about how life just goes on when someone is removed from it. Like Halley died and I still went to school and winter still came and her friends got taller and Mom met George. Like today, I'm not at the Thanksgiving dinner table and everyone is eating and laughing and talking about snowflake dances and gravy. It's like the world pauses for a little bit, and everybody *emotes*, but then just like that life lurches forward. I imagine soldiers, rows and rows of them, marching steadily onward.

At some point, my stomach starts growling. I sit up in bed and the smell of roast turkey and sweet potatoes smacks me.

I'm hungry.

The chatter has turned to murmuring, which means they've all moved into the living room. Which means it's safe to go and forage for food.

Halfway down the stairs, I pause and assess the situation.

There they all are. Poppy dramatically asleep, arms and legs flung out starfish style. Virginia on the floor, texting and grinning. Virginia's mom looking somehow rounder, sitting on Mom's favorite chair, clearly uncomfortable. And there's Mom and George, sitting super close on the couch, his arm draped casually across her shoulders. He's taken off the suit jacket and rolled up his shirtsleeves and his face is pink and his lips are moving and Mom is gazing up at him. I try to figure out which words floating above my bed were about George. *Snowflake dance? Temperamental? Gravy?*

I continue down the rest of the stairs, through the dining room, noting the carnage on the table—turkey bones and red-and-orange-smeared plates and thick globs of congealed gravy on the white tablecloth with colorful autumn leaves dancing across the hem. The smells of different foods mixed together makes me queasy, but I keep going into the kitchen where, lined up all pretty and shimmering, my pies sit, mostly untouched. A sliver of pumpkin is missing, a wedge of apple. Someone has decapitated the meringue tips from the lemon meringue.

They are so beautiful, these pies. The crusts are tender and buttery and flaky and browned just right because the two I burned slightly I threw away.

I pick up the pumpkin pie and the apple and the pecan. I grab a fork from the silverware drawer and then I sit at the kitchen table, which is sticky with spilled cranberry sauce and slippery from butter, and I start to eat. I plunge the fork into the pumpkin first. The filling is smooth and light, rich with vanilla and ginger and cinnamon and nutmeg. I measured all of those spices so carefully and simmered them with pumpkin puree. I whipped milk and cream and eggs and extra yolks and vanilla. I can taste all the care I put into this pie, and I eat it up, one forkful after another, until there are just scraps of crust left.

Without hesitating, I push that pie plate aside and go to work on the apple. Do you know how long it takes to peel, quarter, and core four pounds of Granny Smiths? To zest lemons and oranges? The spices sting my tongue, in a good way. Cinnamon, nutmeg, and allspice. The apples are firm but soft at the same time, and their juices have made, like, a light sauce. In no time, I've finished it, too.

I reach for the pecan. The filling was so simple. Just corn syrup and pecans, brown sugar and butter, a little vanilla, three eggs. The first bite makes my teeth shiver from sweetness. This would be very good with whipped cream, I think. There's whipped cream in the fridge. Not the kind in a can, but fresh whipped cream that I made just for the pecan pie. But I can't stop eating long enough to go and get it and in no time my teeth have adjusted, and I have finished this delicious, sweet pie, too.

"Clementine?" my mother says in a voice that sounds like she's not actually sure it's me.

I look up.

Everyone—Mom, George, Virginia, Celeste, Virginia's mom, a sleeping Poppy draped across her mother's arms—is standing there staring at me.

My lips are sticky. I can feel pie on my face. There are crumbs in my hair.

"What . . . ," Mom begins. She swallows hard and I can practically see her thinking, the wheels inside her head spinning.

"Of course, you must be starving!" she says. "You slept right through dinner!"

This does not defuse the awkwardness in the air between me and all of them.

"You ate three whole pies?" Virginia said, taking a step back, away from me.

I glance at the table where there are three empty pie plates. "I guess so."

"Well, we were just coming in for some ourselves," Mom says cheerfully, bustling into the kitchen and taking plates down from the cupboard and forks out of the drawer. "Good thing you didn't eat *all* the pies. Good thing you saved some for the rest of us."

George takes her cues and approaches the pies.

"Can you believe it?" Mom says. "Clementine made all these pies herself."

"Amazing!" George says.

Virginia's mom picks up their cues. "Well, I told her I was craving pie."

"I'll serve!" George offers.

Slowly, people advance into the kitchen and start giving George their orders. Except Virginia. She hangs back, her thumbs attacking her phone. I feel like I can read her text to Cecily from here. *She ate THREE pies! All by herself!!!*

"Virginia?" George asks. "Pie?"

"I'm good," she says without looking up from her phone.

In no time, they are all pulling up chairs and eating pie with glasses of milk or cups of tea.

"Delicious, Clementine," Virginia's mom says, and everyone agrees and adds compliments upon compliments.

But a person cannot eat three pies safely. I'm starting to feel nauseated, and my stomach is twisting and turning. I try to smile and tell them I'm glad they like the pies.

At some point George says, "I brought a special cognac!"

Then Mom is putting little glasses that we never use on a tray and once again they all move as a group, this time out of the kitchen, the glasses rattling delicately on the tray.

Except Virginia.

She bends down close to me and says, "Matt Stonie holds the Guinness World Record for pie eating. Twenty pounds of pie in eight minutes. I just looked it up."

I don't answer her because my throat is suddenly, violently, clogged with pie rising up from my stomach. Thick and strangling and sweet and sour at the same time. I try to swallow, but there's too much pie, rising like the Mississippi River when it flooded last spring and we had to watch the videos in school. It was roiling and dark, the way the pie feels in my throat.

Virginia is staring down at me. I turn to her, and when I do, I cannot contain the rising Mississippi River and it comes shooting out of my mouth, choking me as maybe twenty pounds of pie fly through the air and right onto Virginia. There are chunks of apples and pecan halves and bright orange all over her skirt and legs and shoes.

A strange calm fills me once all of the pie is out, even as Virginia starts to yell at me, crying and calling me all sorts of names. Even as the others rush back in and start yelling, too. Even as Poppy wakes up, opens her mouth, and throws up all over her mother.

Paper towels appear. And sponges. And the wet mop. And a bucket.

People bustle around me, cleaning, wiping, spraying, mopping.

Can Mom honestly tell me now that I haven't ruined everything?

CHAPTER TWENTY-EIGHT

IN WHICH LOVE IS IN THE AIR

Once, when I was maybe nine or ten, I came home from school and in the living room, hanging above the couch, found the biggest, ugliest painting I had ever seen. There was ocean and sand and beach umbrellas, all of the colors kind of neon instead of soft and summery. Mom found me standing in front of it, staring.

"Right?" she said like she was proud of the thing.

I just kept staring.

"Allison and I went to an art fair and this painting really called to me."

The sun looked like the kind a kindergarten kid draws: a triangle in one corner with beams shooting from it. Except *this* sun was more orange than yellow.

"It was a lot, but I bargained her down a bit," Mom said.

The kitchen door opened and banged shut, which meant Halley was home. She took ballet class after school almost every day so always got home after me.

"Hello?" she called, and I could hear her drop her backpack and ballet bag on the floor.

"In here!" Mom told her.

Halley came into the living room, still in her pink tights and black leotard, a weird flowy skirt over them and her sneakers that lit up when she walked. Her bun was drooping, threatening to fall apart. She stood beside me, smelling of sweat and apple juice.

"What is this?" she said. No, demanded.

"Isn't it beautiful?" Mom said dreamily.

Halle turned to look at Mom. "You're joking, right?"

"What do you mean?"

"It's . . ." She struggled for the best word. "Hideous!"

"Hideous?" Mom said. "Hideous means ugly. Or disgusting."

Halley was nodding. "Right. Yup."

Mom blinked at her and then turned to me. "You don't

think it's *hideous*, do you, Clementine?"

"Oh, I do," I said. Then I added, "The sun is orange."

"And the ocean is lime green," Halley said.

Mom took a few steps back, tilting her head for a better look.

"But that's the artist's vision. Like that artist who painted people with their eyes and hands in the wrong place."

I didn't know who that was, but that didn't sound too great, either.

"Can we give it back?" Halley asked.

"It wasn't a gift! I *bought* it!"

"With money?" Halley shrieked.

"Of course with money," Mom said, eyeing the painting. "It does look brighter indoors," she said.

That very afternoon we made an agreement: No big home changes without a vote. Majority rules.

Sparky, we nicknamed it. We endured Sparky for a year or so, then Mom put it in the attic and Halley and I decided not to mention it ever again.

But Mom seems to have forgotten our agreement. Or maybe she thinks that because Halley is gone, she can make big home changes without a vote. Because the week after Thanksgiving, George appeared in the living room and stayed.

George is the opposite of Sparky. Beige and white and gray where Sparky was orange and lime and purple. And Sparky just hung there, being ugly and bright. George talks. A lot. George takes up space. When I'm in the living room with him, I feel like there's no oxygen. George has it all.

Just like the day Sparky appeared, I came home from school on the Monday after Thanksgiving—expulsion officially over—and found George sitting on the couch, knitting.

I stood in the doorway, feeling like I had somehow landed in the wrong house. Where was Mom? And why was George sitting there?

He looked up and when he saw me, jumped to his feet and shook my hand with his creepy soft one.

"Good to see you," he said, which was weird because what did he expect? He was sitting on my couch in my living room. Of course he was going to see me.

"Where's Mom?" I asked him, pulling my hand out of his buttery grip.

"Upstairs," he said, sitting back down and picking up his knitting again. "Making herself beautiful."

I didn't want to think about it. I wanted George to leave.

Mom swept into the room, wearing a striped dress I'd never seen before.

"Oh good, you're home," she said, happy to see me.

And from that day forth, George has taken Sparky's place. Oh, he goes home around ten o'clock every night, after Mom makes a dinner from a recipe she's found online—sour cream chicken enchiladas, linguine with lemon sauce, baked cod with miso bread crumbs—and the two of them go to the living room and sip one of those tiny glasses of his cognac. For one thing, Mom has never been much of a cook. She does fine with the basics. Spaghetti. Tacos. Roast chicken. Now she's acting like she's the star of a Food Network show, blending things in the blender and toasting spices and nuts and zesting citrus fruit.

Part of me is glad she's doing so much again—her temperature blanket and working at Forget-Me-Knot and cooking complicated dinners. I mean, making those pies was the happiest I've felt in a long time. But a bigger part of me wants her to be the other Mom. The spaghetti with jarred sauce Mom. The *Top Chef: Houston* Mom. The Mom without a boyfriend whose only other person was me.

One night a few days after George appeared on the couch, I walked in the living room after dinner hoping to watch something on TV other than news or sports. But instead of finding them sipping their brandy with Anderson Cooper in the background, I found them making out. George was clutching Mom and she was clutching him back, like they were trying not to drown. Their faces were smooshed together and without thinking I said, "Oh no!"

They pulled apart slowly, like two pieces of taffy stuck together.

Mom looked dazed. George looked sweaty.

"I thought you were upstairs doing your homework!" Mom said, her face as red as the color Rage in her temperature blanket.

"This is so gross!" I yelled, and ran up the stairs.

Later, after George left, Mom knocked on my door.

"Want to talk?" she said.

"No," I said. "I want to disappear."

"That was pretty embarrassing," Mom said, sitting on my bed.

I wasn't sure if she meant embarrassing for her or me.

"The thing is, sweetie," she started. Then she took a big breath and blew it out real slow. "The thing is, George and I are kind of in love."

"Kind of in love?"

Her face is red again. "No. Not kind of." She covers her red face in her hands. "This is so hard, Clementine."

"You think it's hard? How do you think I feel? My whole family is gone!"

She drops her hands, looking horrified. "No, kiddo. I'm right here."

"No, you're not," I say.

Since I didn't want to go home after school and sit around with George, I started hanging out after dismissal. The school has a whole different personality once classes end. There are kids toting trombones and flutes and clarinets. There are kids in the auditorium rehearsing *Rent*, singing "Seasons of Love," over and over and over. There are girls with field hockey sticks and volleyballs running around, and there are kids in the library playing chess and Catan.

Since I don't play an instrument, or a sport, or a game, and I can't sing or dance or emote, I couldn't find a place to fit into. So I just wandered, observing and taking notes. Until two Mondays after George appeared on our couch. Then I found it.

⌖

I'm kind of lurking in the hall, watching the school newspaper kids put together the week's issue. *The Bee* is run by a tyrannical girl named Brooklyn who wants to go to Princeton. She even wears a Princeton T-shirt. Brooklyn is always berating her reporters and rewriting all their stories and rejecting photos. More than once, I've seen her make someone cry. Monday afternoon outside the *Bee* office, when they're closing the week's paper, is maybe my favorite place to be after school.

Out of nowhere, a boy appears and comes and stands

next to me. He has a man bun and gray eyes and he's holding a skateboard. He smells exotic, like something I've never smelled before. I both want to get closer and inhale him and want to move away from him. I do neither. I just watch Brooklyn call a freshman incompetent.

"What are we doing here?" the boy asks me.

"I don't know what *you're* doing here, but I'm watching the Brooklyn show," I tell him. "That freshman is going to cry in three, two . . ."

Right on cue, the incompetent freshman starts to cry and flees the room.

"Good call," he says. Then he adds, "Poor kid. Should we help her?"

"The strange thing is, they like having Brooklyn be mean to them. It's a badge of honor or something."

"Interesting," he says. "So you come here every day—"

"Just Mondays. That's when they close an issue."

"What do you do on Tuesdays?"

I shrug. "Depends. Band practice can be fun."

"*Band* practice?"

"'Eye of the Tiger,' 'Live and Let Die,' and 'In the Mood,'" I say, naming all the songs they're practicing.

"However, the Catan Club can be entertaining. A nasty bunch."

"Withholding wool and bricks and the like?"

"Exactly."

The boy turns to face me. "In other words," he says, "you're also avoiding going home."

"Exactly," I say again.

"Logan," he says.

"Clementine."

And just like that, I fall in love.

CHAPTER TWENTY-NINE

IN WHICH SECRETS ARE NOT REVEALED

"There are better places to avoid home than the corridors of school," Logan says, unnecessarily.

We are sitting on a ledge jutting out from the rocks we just climbed, overlooking a pond. It took us almost an hour to walk here through bramble. My ankles are all scratched up and, even though it's chilly, I'm sweating from the climb.

"I never even knew this was here," I say, looking down at the pond.

"Dead Fish Pond. So named because—"

"I think I get it," I say.

Logan nods, throws small pebbles at the pond. Some land with a distant plop, but most fall too short.

"Question," I say. "Why have I never seen you before?"

"Answer," he says, and I feel my cheeks get hot. "Today was my first day."

"You just moved?"

"I'm always just moving," he says. "The best place we lived was Maine, right near the ocean. That's where my mother is from, so she goes back there a lot when things get bad."

He holds up his hand and counts off on his fingers. "Born there. Went to kindergarten and first grade. Fourth grade. Sixth grade. Eighth grade."

"That's a lot of moving," I say. "I've lived in the exact same house since I was born."

"Sounds pretty nice," Logan says. "But Maine is kind of like that for me. My grandma is there and she feels like home to me."

"How did you know Dead Fish Pond?"

"This is where we lived when I was in fifth grade," he says. "I used to come and hide here."

I don't know what to say, so I stay quiet.

"Who goes first?" he says.

"You mean, jump?" Even as I say it, I'm wondering if

I'll do it. If he says, *yes, let's jump in Dead Fish Pond*, will I actually jump?

"In there? Are you kidding?" he says. "If fish can't live in it, I sure don't want to try."

I know I should feel relieved, but I feel disappointed. I realize that I wanted to do it, to stand at the very edge of this ledge and throw myself into the air.

"I mean who wants to tell the story of their terrible childhood first?" Logan says. "Reveal the reason we would rather walk for an hour to a polluted pond than go home."

Even with all the tragedy that has struck my family, I don't think I had a terrible childhood. I had Spaghetti Fridays, sleepovers at Virginia's house, Morning Glory Montessori, Mom. Halley.

So I say, "You go."

"Okay," he says, narrowing his eyes and looking out beyond the pond. "No father—"

"Me too!" I say with too much enthusiasm, like I just won something.

Instead of thinking I'm inappropriate, he laughs. "The fatherless children club," he says.

I smile at him, hoping he doesn't notice how my top

lip is kind of sticking to my front teeth because I'm kind of nervous. I could really use some water.

"Where's yours?" Logan asks me.

"Dead." That also comes out wrong, so I add, "I was really little. I don't even remember him."

"It's better that way, maybe," Logan says. I can tell he's weighing whether it's better than whatever happened to his father. Then he nods. "I wish I didn't remember my father. He's a real jerk."

"He's alive?"

"As far as I know. He used to show up from time to time, but he hasn't been around in a while. Not that I totally blame him. My mother is . . . not well."

I immediately think of cancer. Of his mother in a dark room, lying in bed, suffering nobly.

"She's in and out of hospitals," Logan is saying, and I think of IVs and chemotherapy and oxygen masks. "*Mental* hospitals," he adds.

My mind goes blank, all the images of his poor mother wasting away gone. *Mental* hospitals.

"It can get pretty bad," he says softly.

Suddenly I can feel the cold leaching into me, into my

bones and even deeper. I shiver and rub my hands up and down my arms.

"Okay," he says after a few minutes. "You now."

The sky is darkening, a steel gray settling over the pond.

I think that some part of me had been ready to tell him everything—about my dad, about Halley and what I did and how it felt to be so dead inside. But I can't do that now. *Mental* hospitals is hanging in the air between us.

"My mom has this boyfriend," I say. That *is* part of my story, just not the biggest part. "George."

"George," he says, rolling his eyes.

"She didn't even really tell me about him, and the next thing I know he's at Thanksgiving and now he's practically living with us."

I try to convince myself that I'm not actually lying to Logan. This is all true. Just not what really matters.

"That stinks," Logan says, and I can't tell if he's disappointed in what I told him, if he wanted more drama, more pain.

"It's like I don't even belong in my own house anymore," I say, surprised by just how true this is.

"So you watch Brooklyn yell at people and listen to

kids singing the songs from some musical," he says.

"I think she's going to marry him," I say for the first time out loud.

"What do your siblings say about George?"

I look straight into his eyes. Logan is a blank slate. It's his first day at our school. He knows absolutely nothing about me.

"I'm an only child," I say.

Logan grins. "We are in the Only Child Fatherless Children's Club then."

It's dark enough to erase the pond and the trees around it, so I feel like the two of us are floating in nothingness, in gray together, suspended above the rocks on our perch.

"Do you have a boyfriend?" Logan says, his voice almost a whisper.

I shake my head. But then in case he can't see me I whisper back, "No."

"How can that be possible? In just one day I can see you're the most interesting person in that whole dumb school. Maybe in the whole state. Maybe even in the whole world."

I feel my cheeks turn hot again and am grateful for the

dark. I don't want him to see me blushing.

"No secrets between us, okay?" Logan is saying.

I can feel the secrets I haven't told him piling up already, but I say, "No secrets."

"How many boys have you kissed?" he asks me.

I think of Jayden in the hall at Miles's house that night. His WANNA HANG? texts at Thanksgiving. Maybe he doesn't count, I think.

"None."

"None? Really?"

"Really," I say.

"Let me get this straight. If you were to let me kiss you here above Dead Fish Pond, that would be your first kiss?"

"Yes," I lie.

My heart is beating so loud I'm worried Logan can hear it.

"How about you?" I manage to ask him.

"Three. Do you hate me? Do you think I'm terrible?"

I laugh. "I don't know yet."

"The first one was Jackie Bates, sixth grade, in the coat closet after school. Then there was Midge Sullivan, eighth grade, first love—"

I hate Midge Sullivan.

"—broke my heart. But lots of kissing. Then I kind of went out with Lacy—"

"Lacy of Lacy and Casey?" I blurt.

"The very one. It was short and sweet."

"But I thought you just moved here?"

"It was during the summer, at this camp in Maine."

I swallow hard. "Lots of kissing?"

"A medium amount," he says.

"Do you still love Midge Sullivan?" I ask him.

"I don't think so. Her family moved to Orlando."

It's darker still. Logan looks almost like a silhouette.

"Why are we talking about Midge Sullivan?" he says.

"Because you kissed her so much."

He leans close, close enough that I can make out his features more closely.

"May I?" he's asking, and I'm not sure, but I think maybe I kissed him first and I feel like I am flying off that ledge and floating above Dead Fish Pond, floating above everything. I throw the words *mental hospital* and *no secrets* and *first kiss* and *only child* out into the nothingness and let them blow away. Like stardust. Like dandelion fluff. Poof! Gone!

With our phone flashlights lighting the way, we make it back down those rocks and through the woods, my free hand in Logan's the whole way. He lives in the opposite direction of me so we part and I walk the rest of the way home alone, still floating.

When I open the door, my mother scares me half to death, practically charging at me, her face bright red and her eyes wild.

"Where have you been?" she's screaming at me.

George is hovering behind her, looking terrified.

Mom is crying, has been crying because her eyes are puffy and also red.

But as soon as she yells at me, she's pulling me into a hug and crying into my hair.

"I thought you . . . ," she says over and over, but no matter how many times she says it she can't finish the sentence.

After what seems like a very long time, she lets me go, but immediately grabs my shoulders and holds me out at arm's length.

"Once you lose a child," she begins, but then she shakes

her head and drops her hands from my shoulders.

"Mom, I'm so sorry," I say, even though the impact of what she was thinking all this time can't be fixed with an *I'm sorry*. I know that.

"Come sit," George says, guiding her to the couch.

"We were about to call the police," Mom says. "George kept saying, 'Give her a little more time, she probably just got involved with something at school,' but I told him, 'Things happen to us. You don't understand.'"

I rush over to her and sit on the floor by her feet. "I just went for a walk," I say. "I lost track of time."

"A walk?" Mom says from the couch. "It's after seven o'clock. School finishes at three. You walked for four hours?"

"No, I sat, too."

"You didn't even answer your phone," she says.

Mom drops her head into her hands as if to say that this is more than she can take.

How can I explain to her that these were the best four hours of maybe my whole life? If Virginia were still my best friend, I'd run upstairs and call her and tell her every detail, starting with Brooklyn and the newspaper kids and ending with how it felt to hold his hand the whole way back. But Virginia isn't my best friend anymore. She's Cecily's.

I tell Mom how sorry I am again and George brings her one of those little glasses of cognac and I go up to my room without even taking off my coat. I hear their voices from beneath me, the hum of fear and relief coming right through the floor.

My phone buzzes. A text from Logan.

Is GEORGE there?

Of course.

He sends me angry-face emojis and I send him laughing emojis and he sends me winking kissing emojis and I send him a beating heart.

Then I lie down on my bed, except I'm not lying down on my bed because I'm still floating. I feel my heart beating and I feel my breath going in and out of my lungs and even though the voices below me keep humming, all I can think is that this is what it feels like to be alive.

CHAPTER THIRTY

IN WHICH I AM HAPPY, FOR ONE WEEK

DECEMBER

I decide the orange hat brought me luck. The day I decided to wear it and to reinvent myself, some things changed for the better. Unfortunately, that was also when George arrived on the scene and Virginia kind of left my life. (Note to self: This is still to be determined, but do I want a Virginia like the one who came for Thanksgiving?) But the orange hat made me feel different about myself. And that led me to walk the corridors of school after dismissal. And that led me to meet Logan. Not that a boy is responsible for my happiness. It's more that I could be myself with someone again. I guess I could say the same about Jude Banks except grief is what made us friends and grief is the very thing I'm trying to escape. And there's Miles, I suppose. But Miles is more of a friend, something I need desperately.

Logan is different.

After our first afternoon at Dead Fish Pond, he is just always with me. He waits for me outside school in the morning and he sits with me at lunch and after school every afternoon we walk back to Dead Fish Pond and sit on the ledge and talk and talk until it gets too dark to see each other and we have to go back.

"Tell me something I don't know about you yet," Logan says on our second afternoon together.

I try to think of something impressive, something true.

"My mother wanted to homeschool but instead she settled for sending us to a Montessori school. Do you know about Maria Montessori?"

Logan tilts his head. "Us?" he asks.

I look at him. And I almost tell him. The words are right there, trying to get out. But I can't do it. I want to be a different girl, someone who doesn't have a dead sister, someone who isn't so broken.

"My best friend Virginia and me," I say easily. "I mean,

my *former* best friend. She has totally changed lately. Our families did everything together. Until she moved to Vermont."

He nods. "Maria Monte . . . ?"

Relieved, I say, "Montessori," and tell him all about Maria Montessori and how she developed her philosophy of education in Italy in the early 1900s. "Basically we did things like pouring and scooping, and gluing paper, and washing windows, and buttoning, buckling, and zipping stuff."

"The teacher made you wash windows?" Logan says, shaking his head. "It sounds like you were just doing her chores!"

"Maria Montessori thought the most valuable tasks kids could learn were the ones they could do at home. Something simple like washing windows does all sorts of things, like show you how water disperses and how to do two things at once and—"

"Okay, okay, I get it," Logan says, lifting his arms like he's giving himself up for arrest. "That does help explain why you're so . . ."

It takes forever for him to finish his sentence.

"Uniquely wonderful," he finally says.

Uniquely wonderful. Not weird, or worse.

"I was thinking of a real secret, something you haven't told me yet, or maybe that you've never told anyone?" Logan continues. "Though I appreciate the lesson on Maria Montessori."

The list of things I haven't told him unfurls in front of me. There I am watching my sister in an ambulance. There I am in the hospital with Mom, crying over Halley. There I am at her funeral, and afterward in her room sniffing her pillow and her pajamas and pulling fine strands of her hair from her hairbrush.

But to Logan there is no Halley.

So I say, "My only deep dark secrets are things I think. Like, for a while I wanted to be a tree."

I leave out that I was in a "special program" at Sandy Point at the time, and that wanting to be a tree sent me into bed long enough for them to kick me out.

Logan sighs, and at first I think he's disappointed again, but then he says, "I love trees. I mean, trees are the coolest things on the planet. Redwoods. Cypress. Even your everyday oaks."

"I like weeping willows," I say.

"Once, when I was super little, my family took the only vacation we ever went on. We rented a camper, the kind that sits on the back of a pickup truck, and drove cross-country. Most of it was hell because, well, my parents. But the best part was when we drove right through a giant sequoia somewhere in California. My father got out and took a picture of me in the truck *in* the tree, hanging outside the window with this big grin on my face. I keep that picture right by my bed, to remind me that there were at least a few minutes when I was actually happy as a kid."

I take his hand and we just sit like that for a really long time.

⌁

After English on Day Three after that first afternoon at Dead Fish Pond, Miles waits at the classroom door for me and asks if I'm going on the field trip.

"Field trip?"

"To see *Raisin in the Sun*? At Playhouse Rep?"

"That must have been announced while I was expelled," I say.

"You can still sign up," Miles says. "It's this Saturday."

I wonder if on Saturday Logan and I will spend all day at Dead Fish Pond. I wonder if he is my official boyfriend and what that means about making plans on the weekends.

"You get extra credit if you go," Miles is saying. "I guess because it's on a Saturday."

"Okay, yeah, I'll go."

Miles nods toward Ms. Quigley's desk. "The sign-up sheet's over there."

We walk together over to the desk where there is indeed a sign-up sheet. I see Jayden's name on it, and Lacy's and Casey's. I try not to think of Logan with Lacy at a camp in Maine as I sign my name.

"Want to come over after school? My parents hosted a fundraiser at the house last night and there's mountains of leftover food. Like crab puffs and mini quiches and shrimp cocktail."

"I can't today," I say.

Miles flicks bangs out of their eyes and says, "We could binge-watch *Friends* or something."

"*Friends*?" I say. "My mother likes that show."

"I think it's funny," Miles says, a little embarrassed.

"Anyway, I've got stuff."

"Okay. Never mind. I can eat a lot of crab puffs on my own."

I realize in that instant that Miles is lonely. They live in this enormous house and are unsure who they are exactly. Like I am.

But Miles is already walking away. I consider calling, "Pamplemousse!" but Logan is coming around the corner and I temporarily forget all about everything else.

"Hey," Logan says.

"Hey."

He takes my fingers in his hands and kind of rubs them and I think I may faint.

"I have work this afternoon," he says, "so—"

"You have a job?" I don't know anyone my age with an actual job, and it seems so adult and important.

"Don't get too impressed," he says. "I just stock shelves at East Side Market."

"I find that impressive," I tell him. "Employment is impressive."

He laughs. "Anyway, I've got to run, but I wanted to

find you and say hi and . . ." And just like that he kisses me real quick. "And do that," he says.

Then he leaves me standing in the hall, dizzy.

$$\rightthreetimes$$

When I get home, I find a note from Mom telling me that she and George are going out for dinner. There's leftover beef stroganoff in the fridge, she writes. She signs the note with a heart.

It feels great to be in the house alone. It feels weird that Mom is on a date. It feels weird that our leftovers are *beef stroganoff.*

I sit on the couch and turn on the television, flipping through the millions of channels and wondering how with so many channels there is not one thing I want to watch. It's dark out and the house is kind of dark, too, and I start thinking about the times Mom used to go out and leave Halley and me alone, which wasn't often. She would make macaroni and cheese for us and put on a movie and make us promise to not touch anything or go anywhere. "Just sit until I get back, okay?" she'd say. We used to tease her about it, but she would take us in her arms, both of us at once, and say, "You are my most precious treasures. I don't know what I'd do if anything happened to you."

Then something did. The worst possible thing.

That feeling starts washing over me. It doesn't have a name, but it's grief and sadness and anger all wrapped together, and it makes me want to do bad things.

My heart is racing, and I jump up from the couch and try to think about what I can do to stop all the thoughts rushing at me.

Like a message from heaven or somewhere, a text pops up on my phone. It's a picture of crab puffs and shrimp cocktail and a can of grapefruit LaCroix, and that's all it takes. I text Mom that I'm going to Miles's house and then I'm putting on my coat and out the door.

People have started putting up Christmas decorations. Blue lights twinkle from one set of hedges, white from another. There's a Santa in his sleigh on the roof next door and across the street is a giant nativity. It doesn't feel right, all these Christmas decorations. All this *joy*. Funny, down the street, in someone's yard, there's actually the word JOY written in multicolored lights, blinking at me.

The clouds open up and send a flurry of snow into the night. Small, tiny flakes fall fast and hard all around me, immediately sticking to the ground and to me. By the time Miles answers the door, I look like the abominable snowman, snow covered and monster-ish.

"I hear you have shrimp cocktail?" I say through my chattering teeth.

Miles looks surprised, but just lets me in and runs to grab a towel and sweatshirt for me. When I emerge from the bathroom, combed and dried, there's a buffet of leftover food. We get to work on it, the mini quiches and crab puffs and scallops wrapped in bacon held together with curly-topped toothpicks. Shrimp cocktail and mini duck tacos. Baked brie topped with some kind of jelly. These are definitely the best leftovers I have ever had.

I can't help but notice that Miles's house is also ready for Christmas. But unlike my neighborhood, here it looks like a professional Christmas decorator came and set about matching every single thing. All the lights are soft and white, and everything else is silver—bells and tinsel and statues of angels almost as big as I am. Enormous silver pots of white poinsettias are strategically placed and on windowsills there are silver pots, each with a single white orchid in it.

"My mother absolutely loves Christmas," Miles says apologetically.

"It's nice," I say.

But I'm thinking about our Christmas tree with all the homemade decorations and the macaroni wreaths spray-painted gold and the strands of shiny red-and-blue garland strung everywhere. Last year, Mom and I couldn't bear to put up a tree. Or do anything Christmas-y. I wonder what we'll do this year? I decide that tomorrow I will get the boxes of Christmas decorations and I will hang that garland and those macaroni wreaths and I'll put out the candlesticks shaped like fat, jolly snowmen.

"Do you want to stay over? It's snowing pretty hard," Miles asks me, and I look at them, surprised.

"We have *three* guest rooms," they continue. "And a closet filled with pillows so you can have whichever kind you prefer. Goose down, foam, soft, firm. Anything."

"You have a closet just for extra pillows?"

"Then we can go to the play from here tomorrow," Miles offers.

"I'll have to check with my mom."

"Okay. Check?"

I text Mom, and while I wait for her to answer I say, "I'm not sure, but I think I have a boyfriend." Miles is one of my favorite people in the whole world and I don't want to break their heart.

Miles looks confused for a minute, but then laughs and shakes their head. "I'm not, like, hitting on you. In fact—" they lower their voice "—I have a crush on someone, too."

I surprise myself by feeling kind of hurt.

"Jayden," Miles whispers.

"Jayden the scholar athlete?" I blurt.

Miles's cheeks are bright red, but they're grinning a little. "I know, I know. Lacy. Or Casey."

I grin, too, loving that they mix those two up. Loving that Miles and I are *friends*.

My phone dings. "Good idea! It's snowing like crazy!"

"Okay," I say.

"Okay what?"

"Let's go pick out my pillow."

CHAPTER THIRTY-ONE

IN WHICH I AM A TERRIBLE PERSON

When I get home from *A Raisin in the Sun*, I find Mom and George in the living room trying to center a really tall tree in the tree holder. Its branches are fat and vaguely bluish. I watch them working together like that, Mom holding the center of the tree and George on his knees under it, adjusting and readjusting. They are laughing as they do it. *Happy* is the word that comes to mind. Even though I want Mom to be happy, even though I know how much she deserves to be happy, I can't get rid of the nut of resentment lodged in my gut. For my whole life, it was me and Halley and Mom facing everything together. Without Halley here, and with George in the picture, I can't figure out how I fit in. I haven't even figured out yet who I am without Halley, and all of a sudden I have to figure out who I am without Mom.

Mom and George stand back to admire it and that's when they see me.

"Not bad, huh?" Mom says to me, her face flushed.

"It's okay," I say.

"Wait until you see the ornaments we got!" she says, and George says he'll go get them and bustles out to the car.

"Ornaments? We already have ornaments," I remind her.

"I know, sweetie. But I don't want George to feel left out so we went to Crate & Barrel and picked out a few new ones."

George comes back in and he has two shopping bags, which is a lot for a few ornaments.

"Remember the ones Halley and I made of our hands at Morning Glory?" I hold up my hand as if that might jog her memory. "We wrote our names on them," I add.

"Of course, I remember," Mom says. "And I'm going to go up to the attic and get them as soon as we show you these."

She starts pulling tissue-wrapped ornaments out of one of the bags. One is a bowl of spaghetti and another is of a taco, all shiny and new.

"For Pasta Fridays and Taco Sundays," Mom says, and my heart floods with something I can't describe. Maybe it's longing or sadness. Or happiness.

The next ones she unwraps are all made to look like old-fashioned ones, frosted and striped and also shiny.

"Oh," Mom says, "and we got those lights that flash on and off."

She burrows through the bags, I guess looking for the lights.

"We have lights," I say. "The ones that look like snowflakes and those tiny twinkly ones."

"The tree is just so big," George says, "we figured we might need more."

George. I forgot he was here. The sound of his voice and his pink skin and white socks and new ornaments and flashing lights are too much for me. I leave without saying anything to get the ornaments, *our* ornaments, the *real* ornaments.

It takes me a while to find them and then to move

the boxes down to the living room, and when I get there Mom and George are actually putting the spaghetti and the taco *on* the tree. They've already strung the lights and they are blinking on and off like we're in a disco and I do the only thing I can think of, I pick up the old-fashioned-looking ornaments that Mom has laid out on the coffee table and I sweep them off the table, sending them to the floor. At least one of them breaks, but I wish all of them would break. I feel like a little kid, doing something like that. I feel upset and embarrassed and like I'm about to cry.

George stands with his mouth dropped open, and I turn to Mom but she has taken the ornament of Halley's five-year-old hand out of a box and she is staring at it with the saddest look of pain and love all mixed together, and then she sits down right there under the tree and presses that plaster-of-paris hand to her chest and starts to weep.

"I'm sorry," I say.

I realize George thinks I'm apologizing about the new ornaments because he's saying *It's okay, it's okay*, and rushing off to get a broom. But I'm apologizing for making Mom cry, for not thinking about how seeing Halley's little five-year-old's hand would break her heart all over again.

"Mom, I'm sorry," I say, kneeling beside her. "I didn't mean to make you cry."

"I know," she says softly. Her crying is stopping but she doesn't let go of the ornament. "Does it happen to you, too? You're doing your best, trying to move forward, trying to be happy even, and then out of nowhere something comes and knocks you down? Like this?" she says, holding out the ornament.

"Only every day," I say.

She gives me a sad smile. "Maybe sometimes I try too hard," she says. "Like the tree and everything. Maybe it's still too soon."

"I think it's too soon for me," I admit.

George appears with the broom and dustpan, and this time I do apologize to him.

But he holds up a hand to stop me. "You and your mom are doing your best," he says. "I know it's hard."

I make myself stay and help decorate the tree. And really, it isn't awful. In fact, when we finish and the lights are twinkling at us and the tinsel glitters, it's actually pretty nice.

—≻⊁︎—

Later, up in my room, I remember how Virginia and her family used to always come over on Christmas Day and we'd exchange gifts. The rule was that you could only give gifts you made yourself, like seashells we'd collected at the beach strung on a chain to make a necklace, or pot holders woven on a little plastic loom.

Without thinking, I text Virginia.

Hey stranger!

I'm surprised she texts back right away.

We're decorating our tree! We went and cut it down ourselves.

I roll my eyes. *Vermont.*

But I text:

Wow! Fun!

And I add a Christmas tree emoji.

She sends a Santa emoji. But then goes quiet, even after I tell her we just decorated our tree, too.

I can picture her, my former best friend, and her mom and Celeste, bundled up in Vermont clothes like thick cabled sweaters and UGG slippers. And Poppy crawling around and Jack probably reciting poems from memory.

A text pings and I think: Virginia!

But it's Logan, and it says:

> **Look out your window!!!**

I go over to the window and standing below it, looking up, is Logan.

Instead of opening it and shouting down to him, I pull on my fleece and run downstairs. Christmas carols are still playing, but the room is empty. I grab my jacket and go outside where Logan is waiting.

"Hey," I say.

"Hey," he says back.

Without saying anything else, we start walking around my neighborhood, past all the houses lit with lights.

There are trees in some windows and menorahs in other windows, all of them sending out a warm glow.

"It's nice here," Logan says, sounding sad.

"I guess."

"Do you know all these people in all these houses?"

"Most of them."

He points to a house. "Who lives there?"

"The Ramirezes. They're super old."

He points to another house.

"The Whitneys. They have a million kids," I say.

Logan shakes his head. "I wanted to tell you something," he says, and my heart skips a beat because I know it's something bad.

"I'm going back to Maine," he says.

"But you just got here!"

"I'm going back to live with my grandmother. My mom . . ." He shakes his head again.

"You can't," I say softly.

"We can text and FaceTime and stuff," he says, but I know how that goes from Virginia moving to Vermont. You promise to do it but neither of you does.

"When are you going to leave?"

"I've got a bus ticket for next Saturday."

I kick at some ice that used to be beautiful snow but now has frozen and gotten dirty.

"Hey!" Logan says. "You should come with me!"

I look at him. "To Maine?"

"My grandmother is an amazing cook," he says. "Do you like pancakes? You do, right? She makes the best pancakes."

I go back to kicking the ice.

"Plus," Logan says, "no George."

I think of George in his white socks. He wears them with Birkenstocks around the house, which is not a good look. But it's not a reason to hate a person. Then I remind myself that because of George we have new ornaments on the tree and Mom doesn't act like she used to and I don't fit in at my own house anymore.

"That is a plus," I say.

Then he bends down and we kiss for what feels like a really long time and also too short a time and I forget for a little while about Maine and George and everything else that's bad in my life.

CHAPTER THIRTY-TWO

_⁀⁌⁀_

IN WHICH I AM, BRIEFLY, HAPPY

It's the last week of school before winter break, which means we have lots of assemblies and some teachers let us play Bananagrams or watch a movie instead of doing actual work. Miles talks me into doing tech with them on the drama club's production of _Seussical_. Every day after school we go to the auditorium and paint the set or talk backstage to each other on walkie-talkies about entrances and costume changes and lighting. Lacy plays Mayzie La Bird and Jayden plays Horton the Elephant, and they're actually really good. Lacy has this song called "Amayzing Mayzie" and she wears this sparkly purple dress and an enormous purple-feathered headdress, and she steals the show.

"Look at you," Mom says when I come home at six every night after rehearsal. "You're actually having fun."

Even George doesn't dampen my spirits. I have friends. I'm doing something I like. And I have a boyfriend. Every now and then I get a big pang of guilt. How can I have fun when Halley is dead? How can I feel happy? I remember Gloria telling us one night at City of Angels that this is one of the biggest obstacles to getting through grief. "But, kids," she said, "even though your sister or brother died, you didn't. You're alive and you deserve to be happy." At the time, I couldn't imagine ever being happy again, so I didn't really think about what she said. But this week I do. A lot. Every time I catch myself laughing and then feel that stab of guilt, I make myself remember what Gloria said.

The only bad thing about this week is that Logan is working every night to make money for Maine. He is leaving the day after the play opens. He texts me and sends me heart emojis, but I basically don't see him except for in school. "You coming to Maine with me?" he asks me when we say goodbye after school. "Maybe," I say, though as each day passes the urge to flee lessens.

Thursday night is tech night, which means we have to run through the entire musical twice and be sure every detail is in place. We don't finish until after ten, and I'm outside the school waiting for Mom to pick me up when Lacy comes out. Her character in the play is self-centered and vain and she manipulates anyone she can into doing whatever she wants. Kind of like the real Lacy. Maybe that's why she's so good in the role.

"You were great tonight," I tell her.

"Thanks," she says.

We stand there awkwardly because even though we're in this together, we don't have very much to say to each other.

Then Lacy turns to face me. "What's up with you and Logan, anyway?" she says, and for once she sounds nice to me.

"He's . . . we're . . ."

"Like, going out?" she says. Her eyes get kind of wide and she smiles like she's excited.

"Well, yeah."

"He's adorable," Lacy says.

I wonder if I should tell her that I know about them at camp, but I decide to just let it go. After all, he isn't sending her heart emojis.

"I guess so," I say.

"Do you like him a lot?"

In the distance I see headlights approaching and I hope it's Mom. This conversation has started to make me feel uncomfortable. I mean, Lacy and I are definitely not friends.

"I guess," I say again.

Her face is blank and pretty and she says, "Do you think he likes you? A lot?"

I keep my eyes on the car that's approaching. It is Mom, I realize, relieved.

"I think so?" I tell her. "Here's my mom, so . . ."

"Is that one of your friends?" Mom says when I get in.

I don't tell her that's the girl I slapped back in September.

"She plays Mayzie La Bird," I say.

Even though I wish Logan could come to the show, I have such a good time on opening night. The curtain got stuck and someone forgot to put the spotlight on Eve, the senior who plays Gertrude, for the first few seconds of her singing "Notice Me, Horton," but otherwise it was a big success.

Miles threw the cast party at their house and has buckets of chicken wings from Pluck U and stacks of pizzas and a big cake with a picture of the Cat in the Hat on it. I hang out with Samantha and Miles and sing along when a junior who was in the ensemble sits at the piano and plays show tunes.

"No Logan?" Lacy says to me at some point, and I tell her he's working.

"I don't trust her at all," Samantha says as we watch Lacy walk away.

When eleven o'clock comes and Mom picks me up, I'm actually sad to go. But not as sad as when I get home and Logan texts me:

> Just showed up at the party! Where are you???

I consider asking Mom if she'll drive me back, but the

last thing she said to me was, "I'm so tired I'm about to drop." She's working extra holiday hours at Forget-Me-Knot and even George hasn't been around much this week.

"In bed," I text Logan, and add about a million crying faces.

"So much for surprises," he texts, and sends a million crying faces, too.

He's leaving tomorrow at noon for Maine, and I didn't even get to say a proper goodbye.

> **Come over before your bus tomorrow?**

I wait for him to answer and after what seems like forever dots finally appear. But all I get is a thumbs-up emoji.

I text him some hearts, but he must have found the chicken wings because I don't get any more texts. I send him one more:

> **See you in the morning!!!**

CHAPTER THIRTY-THREE

IN WHICH THE TRUTH COMES OUT

The next morning is one of those winter mornings that are so sunny and bright that the sun makes everything glisten and it all hurts your eyes. Plus, the temperature dropped overnight and even inside I can feel the cold. After I check my phone and find nothing, I put my fleece on over my pajamas and go downstairs.

Mom's on the couch under an afghan she crocheted, drinking coffee and doing the crossword puzzle in the newspaper.

"I thought you'd sleep in after your big week," she says.

"My friend Logan is coming over."

"Now?"

It's almost nine and his bus leaves at twelve.

"Soon," I say, glancing at the clock.

"Are you up for a little talk?" Mom says, and she pats the sofa beside her.

I sit down and put the corner of the afghan over me, too. "Last time you wanted to talk you told me about George," I say.

"Well," she says, and I watch her face rearrange itself. But for what?

"Did you break up?"

"No!" she says, surprised.

"He hasn't been around much," I point out.

"I've been having dinner with him on my breaks," she says.

"Moules?" I tease her.

"Sometimes," she says.

I roll my eyes.

"Actually, sweetie, this is kind of the opposite of breaking up," Mom says.

I try to think of what the opposite of breaking up is, and I don't like where I land.

"George and I want to get married," Mom says before I can blurt out practically the very same thing. "I can't believe I just said that out loud!" she says, and laughs nervously. She takes a big breath. "Phew!"

"Married?" I say.

That thing starts again: I know I should be happy for her, and somewhere inside me I am, but all I can think about is if—no, *when* Mom and George get married, I'll be alone. And what if she's like Virginia's mom and has other children? Then where do I belong?

"You look upset," Mom says, crestfallen.

"He wears white socks. With sandals."

"Sweetie," Mom says.

"Are you going to have other kids? Are you making a new family?" I say, and I'm crying now and wishing my heart could be bigger and open up instead of clenching shut like this.

"Oh, Clementine, *you're* my family. That's why I'm telling you what's going on. I could never replace you. Or Halley. Or even your dad."

"Then why marry somebody?"

"He's not just somebody," Mom says.

"He is to me!" I say.

Mom keeps talking in that sad voice, trying to explain

how nothing will change when I know everything will change, so I go back upstairs and wait for Logan. While I wait, I think about how he asks me every day to go to Maine with him. Holding hands on the way to Maine, eating his grandmother's pancakes, being away from what used to be my home and my family forever but now is something I don't even recognize . . . all of that sounds like a good idea.

I text Logan:

> **It's almost 10! When are you coming?**
> **I have a surprise for you.**

But he doesn't answer. He must be packing, I decide. It takes a lot of time to pack up your whole life.

Mom calls up to me. "I'm off to work, sweetie. You okay?"

"Sure," I say.

"When your friend comes there's frozen waffles."

"Okay!"

At eleven, I text him again:

> **Your bus is at noon, right?**
> **It wasn't earlier?**

Still nothing.

I wait until 11:30 and then I throw underwear and socks and a shirt in my backpack and I run down the stairs and out the door because if I don't make it to the bus station by noon, I may never see Logan again.

⁃⁃⁃

The bus station is busy, filled with people going places for the holidays, I guess. At first, I can't find Logan and I think maybe he did take an earlier bus. But then there he is, already in line for the bus to Boston where he'll connect for Maine.

"Logan!" I call, even as I'm pushing my way through the crowd to him.

He turns around but instead of breaking into a grin like I expected, he looks very unhappy to see me.

I'm finally standing right beside him. "I heard there's some really good pancakes at the end of this trip," I say, keeping my voice light though something is very, very wrong.

"Bus to Boston at gate 8," comes over the loudspeaker. "Boarding."

"What's the matter?" I ask him.

"Oh, nothing. I mean, it's not like *my* sister died and *I* tried to off myself and spent time, like, just last month in some special program for messed-up kids, right?"

"Logan," I say.

But he keeps talking.

"It's not like *I* lied to someone who opened up their heart to me. So yeah. I'm just fine."

I want to explain, but I know I don't have an explanation. I lied about everything. On purpose. To him.

"Who told you all this stuff?"

"Lacy. At the party last night. She couldn't believe that I didn't know anything about my girlfriend."

"Let me explain everything on the bus, okay?" I say, unable to keep the desperation out of my voice.

He looks surprised. "No, Clementine. Not okay. I don't ever want to talk to you again."

The line has started to move, and people are getting on the bus.

I wish Logan wouldn't walk away without saying anything else. But that is exactly what he does. He walks away. He doesn't look back.

CHAPTER THIRTY-FOUR

IN WHICH I REACH

Sometimes I believe that I used up most of my tears when Halley died. But then something happens that reminds me that we poor humans have an endless supply. Like Logan finding out I lied to him. Like Logan telling me he never wanted to talk to me again. I cried for most of the afternoon. Then I just lay there and thought about how all of a sudden, everything had changed. Twenty-four hours ago, I was happy, and now my mother and George were getting married and Logan hated me.

Mom is working a double shift, so I am alone with my miserable self. The house is really quiet. Too quiet.

Except...

I take out my notebook, and write:

Radiator hissing.

House creaking. "It's just settling," Mom used to say.

Wind in trees outside my window.

Ice dripping from roof.

House groaning. "It's just tired, Clementine."

More dripping.

I get up and lift my shade and right out my window, clinging to the very edge of the roof, is an enormous icicle. Even though it's cold and windy outside, it's melting. Big fat drips are plopping off. As I stand there and watch it, the moonlight or streetlight hits it in just the right way and it looks lit up from within, like a beautiful glowing thing.

And I realize something too as I stand there. A few months ago, all of this stuff would've sent me into a tailspin. But right now, instead, I am standing here and seeing something beautiful.

I open the window (screech of window opening) and stick my hand out. But I can't reach the icicle unless I lean way out (sound of me gasping when the cold hits me), stretching, stretching.

A cold drop falls onto my hand (soft plop) and it feels wonderful, icy and surprising.

And I stretch even more and reach even more.

And then, I fall.

(a whoosh, then body hitting snowy ground)

(air knocked out)

(grunt)

And then: "Clementine!" (Mom screaming)

⸙

In the ambulance, they keep asking me questions.

"Who's the president?" the guy asking the questions asks.

"Move your toes for me, sweetheart," the guy checking my body parts says.

"What's your name?"

"Good, good, now move your fingers for me, sweetheart."

I don't answer the guy asking the questions, but I do what the other guy tells me. Wiggle my toes. Bend my fingers. I do it mostly to be sure I'm not paralyzed or something.

Mom is sitting in the front seat next to the ambulance driver. "You can't go back there, ma'am," he said. "No seat belt." Just like when I rode in the ambulance with Halley and they made me sit up front.

Mom got in the front and put on her seat belt and started to cry, which she is still doing. Softly, but I can hear her. I wonder if she is also thinking of the last time someone in our family was taken away in an ambulance? How that person never came home again?

"Tell me what hurts," the guy checking my body parts says. "Head? Back?"

"Yes," I say.

"Head and back?"

"Yes. And leg maybe? And shoulder?"

"What's your name?"

When I don't answer, Mom yells, "Her name is

Clementine and she jumped out of a second-floor window."

"Rotate your ankle for me, sweetheart."

"You jumped out the window?" the guy asking the questions asks me, his voice all serious.

I close my eyes, but the guy checking my body parts says, "Open your eyes for me, sweetheart," so I do, briefly.

"What day is it?" the guy asking the questions asks.

"It's the day she jumped out the window," Mom sobs.

I realize the siren is on and the red light is flashing, like the day they took Halley to the hospital. The guy keeps telling me to wake up, but it is impossible. My eyes feel like they are made of iron. Iron curtains dropping shut.

The next thing I know I'm being bounced out of the ambulance and whisked into the emergency room, Mom jogging beside me. She looks about as worried as I've ever seen her.

The guy who checked out my body parts is barking at the nurses who rush to greet us.

He says *concussed* and *broken* and *jumped.*

Inside my head I'm screaming "I fell!" but the iron curtain is still down, and my voice has disappeared.

"I'll call psych," a nurse says.

I hear Mom start to cry again.

I hear *X-ray, CT scan, psych evaluation.*

Then I hear nothing at all.

That is how I got here to the point where Mom sighs and says, again, "Oh, Clementine. Why?"

For the next three days, that's all I think about. *"Oh, Clementine. Why?"* I go over everything that's happened, and I try to understand my own thinking, my own self.

Concussed means a lot of stuff medically, but if you're the one concussed it means major headache that won't go away and sleeping all the time. Every time I open my eyes, Mom is sitting there knitting and she jumps up and looks down at me with her sad eyes. But I can't tell her this whole big story yet. My head hurts too much and I'm way too tired.

But on the third day, I wake up and my head is only pounding a little bit. This time Mom isn't sitting there, but a nurse is standing over me and she smiles when I look at her.

"Well, hello!" she says.

"Hi."

"You did quite a job on yourself, missy. Concussion. Broken ankle. In two places! Sprained wrist. Whatever were you thinking?"

I look up into her big brown eyes and I say, "I tried to touch this icicle and I fell."

She tilts her head. "Is that right?"

"It was beautiful," I say.

⟶╎⟵

A doctor comes in and I tell her the same story about the noises in the house and the icicle and reaching too far.

"And you fell?" she says.

"I fell."

While I'm eating chicken noodle soup, a group of carolers stands in the doorway of my room and bursts into a too-loud, too-cheerful rendition of "Joy to the World." They are all hospital employees, dressed in various colored scrubs and Crocs. The sound of their voices makes me cry. Not because they sound beautiful or anything. But because I remember reaching for that icicle, and I remember what I was thinking right before I did.

I guess they take my tears for happiness because they pause briefly and then dive right into "Rudolph the Red-Nosed Reindeer." When they sing, ". . . had a very shiny nose," half of them follow by shouting, "A red nose!" And when they sing, ". . . they would really say it glows," half of them shout, "Really glows!" The shouters are so enthusiastic that a passing nurse pauses to see what's going on.

They continue this way, the shouters shouting, "Poor Rudy!" and "No games!"

By the time they finish, with a jingling of actual bells, I realize that maybe they were right. I was happy.

—✳—

Now here I am in this hospital, crying because all of that cheer was sent into my room, and I don't know what to do with it. Outside, snow starts to fall. The flakes are small and fast and they sparkle from the lights in the parking lot. They look like the snow in snow globes, and I think that I'm still in a snow globe, just a different one. Shake it and all that snow falls around a heartbroken girl who is just trying to figure out how to live her life.

I don't know how long I lie watching the snow fall, feeling the limits of that glass globe trapping me inside, before Mom comes in. Her coat and hair are covered with snow and her nose is bright red.

She takes off her coat and shakes it before draping it over a chair.

"Another double?" I ask her, and she nods.

"I would have been here sooner," she says, dropping into the other chair, "but I was waylaid by carolers. Couldn't get past them."

"So cheerful," I mumble in my scratchy voice.

"*Too* cheerful," Mom says.

She leans over me and smooths my hair. It feels nice and I close my eyes.

"I thought you jumped out that window because of George and me," she says softly.

"You know what? Old me might have thought about doing something like that. But I'm different."

"An icicle," she says, shaking her head.

She rearranges herself in the hard chair and digs around in her bag. Then she hands me a wrapped box.

"It's probably too corny," she says, "but ..."

The wrapping paper has smiling snowmen on it and that's when I realize it's Christmas Eve. I should be home drinking Mom's homemade eggnog and cutting out stars and trees for cookies. Mom should be making her most special dinner: little hot dogs wrapped in dough and water chestnuts wrapped in bacon, then a cheesy, gooey lasagna with a Caesar salad, and then those sugar cookies shining with red and green sparkles. Halley should be there with us, but that's not how our lives turned out.

"Go ahead," Mom is saying. "Open it."

I try to unwrap without ripping the paper because Mom likes to reuse it.

But she says, "That paper has been around the block a few times. Don't worry about it."

So, I tear the rest. There's a blue box, and inside lots of white tissue paper, and beneath all of that is a snow globe. A heavy glass one on a dark blue base. I hold it up and see that inside the globe is a picture, a photograph of Halley and me from the summer before she died. We are at the beach cabin we always rented, and our skin is golden, and our hair is wet, and our heads are tilted together. We look happy. Like sisters. My eyes fill with tears, but

I manage to turn the snow globe upside down and then right it so that the snow falls. Except instead of white flakes, tiny gold stars swirl around us, a thick whirlwind of *Can't wait!*

"It's not corny," I manage. "It's perfect."

ACKNOWLEDGMENTS

Endless gratitude to my brilliant editor and friend, Francesco Sedita, who makes anything possible. And thanks to Michael Louis Howard and the entire team at Penguin Workshop for all their hard work. My family supports everything I do, and my love for Michael, Sam, and Annabelle knows no bounds. And, as always, in memory of my Gracie.